The Spa and the Single Mom

THE ROYALS OF SAILFISH BANKS
BOOK ONE

DELANCEY STEWART

MARIKA RAY

Copyright © 2023 by Delancey Stewart / Marika Ray

All rights reserved.

No part of this book may be reproduced in any form or by any electronic or mechanical means, including information storage and retrieval systems, without written permission from the author, except for the use of brief quotations in a book review.

Cover Design: Kelly Lambert Greer

Editing: Evident Ink

Cover Photo: Jane Ashley Converse

Cover Model: Jordan Wheeler

Chapter One
CAVANAUGH

P lotting an assassination would be easier than plotting an escape from the Mardelvia palace. Not a single member of the royal family or the hundreds of staff we employed knew of my plans. I'd kept every detail under wraps, only trusting one man who'd been my friend since I was ten years old.

Emilio and I should never have met that day of our field trip to the tulip gardens. I was a prince. He was a farmer's son. And yet friendship had bloomed despite the urgings of my mother to think of my duty to the crown first. Now I was asking him to fly the small plane that would take me to my uncle's home in America. It could cost Emilio a life sentence in prison if my parents found out he'd helped me.

"We have exactly five minutes to take off or the traffic controller will be back from his smoke break. And I don't have enough cash on me to bribe him to take another one." Emilio didn't waste any time when I emerged from the bulletproof sedan right there on the small runway. I could barely see him in the dim light of the half moon. "Hope you packed light."

"Only brought five of my favorite crowns," I drawled in the American accent I'd been working on for months. Ever since I hatched this plan.

Emilio scoffed, a sound so familiar it made me pause even when I knew we had to hurry.

I would miss the man. Along with every little detail my country had to offer. The cool night air wafted around me and brought the salty brine of the ocean on the breeze. If I'd been a mere citizen, I'd have never left, but being the spare heir to the throne came with complications I just couldn't live with any longer.

Emilio tossed my two duffel bags into the plane and turned back to me. "Last chance to back out, Cav."

I shook my head, squaring my shoulders and steeling myself to do what was necessary. I'd been taught how to stuff down my own desires since the day I was born. It almost came naturally now. "Let's go."

Emilio pulled me into a hug and slapped my back more times than usual. I appreciated that he was the one person in my life who didn't treat me like I was something special. I was just another human in his eyes and I liked it that way. "Happy birthday."

I whacked him on the back just as hard and then let go. "Thanks."

My freedom was the birthday present I'd been dreaming of for the past few years as it became increasingly obvious that it was the one thing I'd never have in my home country.

As I climbed into the plane and strapped in, I wondered what would happen when the palace awoke and the birthday prince was not under its roof. Mother would fret and snap at everyone around her only to go cry in private. Father would grumble and roll his eyes at his son's foolishness. And Archie, my older brother and heir to the throne, would text my personal phone repeatedly, trying to talk me out of whatever shenanigans I'd gotten myself into. Sadly, I'd never get those messages. I'd left all electronics behind, to be found when my parents sent out a search party, along with a letter explaining that I was fine and I'd contact them soon.

Emilio, the best pilot in his graduating class in our military, got the plane up in the air remarkably quickly. As the land below fell away, I gazed at the familiar coastline, the slowly fading lights, saying a silent goodbye to my country and to the people I'd served faithfully for forty years. Guilt fired in my chest, but the siren call of freedom flared brighter.

"Prepare for landing, Cav. It's going to be bumpy."

Emilio's voice in my headphones woke me from sleep. I blinked rapidly and tried to bring my focus back to my plan. Leaving in darkness and arriving in darkness was best for laying low but it was disorienting to travel back in time zones. The older I got, the more traveling and changing time zones seemed to affect me. Yet another reason to leave behind the crown and all the royal duties that life entailed.

The plane landed softly, but as promised, the landing strip

was littered with potholes. I gripped the armrests and reminded myself that this was what I'd signed up for. I was no longer in Mardelvia, that was for sure. Father would never have let our airstrips get this dilapidated. When the plane finally came to a halt outside a hangar that had also seen some hard times, I took the headset off and helped Emilio get things squared away.

"Will your uncle let you stay with him?" Emilio asked as we each grabbed a duffle bag off the plane.

"I'd rather not give you the details, friend. The less you know, the better."

Emilio dipped his head in a nod. He knew I trusted him. Less details meant he would be charged with less should anyone find out his part in this. "I will refuel and head to the Bahamas for a few days. Shame I forgot my phone, though."

I shot him an appreciative grin. "Enjoy the rum. Maybe the ladies too, no?"

Emilio eyed the lone truck ambling toward us. Uncle Leo said he'd swing by in a truck to pick me up so I wasn't worried. Besides, no one else knew I was here. I was any other Joe Blow on a tarmac, shooting the shit, as the Americans would say. I did not understand why anyone would shoot bullets at shit, but then again, Americans were a different breed.

"Call me in a few days if you need anything. I should be back in Mardelvia by then." Emilio gave me one last hug, pulling back to study my face.

"I'll be okay, mother." Teasing was better than admitting that I had a lump in my throat too. I wasn't sure when I'd see my best friend again.

"Fuck off, Barclay," Emilio grumbled right back before handing me the duffle bag and walking back to his plane without a backward glance. Neither of us were big on displays of emotion.

A truck door slammed and I looked over to see a tall silver-haired man leaning against the hood, directly in the pool of light shining down from the one flood light mounted on the hangar. He had on worn jeans, a pair of leather boots, and a sky blue polo shirt. His face held quite a bit of unruly beard, but his blue eyes snapped with vitality. He looked exactly like my father, if Father had ever donned a pair of jeans instead of suit pants.

"Uncle?" I called out.

He lifted a hand and I walked over, excitement for the adventure ahead drowning out the guilt and sorrow. "That's your outfit for blending in around here?"

I looked down at my black slacks and button-down shirt. It was my most casual outfit, aside from my riding clothes and I didn't think jodhpurs were appropriate for this mission. "Perhaps we need to go shopping."

He scoffed and it sounded exactly like my father. "Come here, boy."

He pulled me into a back-breaking hug, laughing jovially. I barely knew my own uncle, to be honest. He never visited Mardelvia, seeing how he'd left the royal life and settled in the United States, which was exactly the plan I had in mind. My parents had allowed us boys to visit him in North Carolina a few times over the years, always with a stern lecture about his life being the path not to take. I couldn't understand why, when he was so happy living life in a house almost as big as the palace, and had a boat he took us out on during the hottest days of the summer. Seemed like a nice life to me.

We piled in the truck while Uncle Leo talked my ear off

about everything going on with him and my cousins. I answered him when necessary while mostly having my nose against the window looking out at the landscape. It was hot here and more humid than Mardelvia, but there was something wild and free in the air that fed the energy pumping through my veins.

"We can get you some clothes and boots at the Wally, and then hit up my favorite diner for some dinner," Uncle Leo finally offered as we left some of the traffic behind. The flicker of the ocean to our right drew my eye.

"Sure." I had no idea what Wally was but if that's where Uncle Leo wanted to go, I was up for the adventure.

Uncle Leo flicked a glance in my direction every few seconds. "You sure your parents are okay with you visiting?"

I hoped my answer wouldn't ruin my visit before it had even begun. "Actually, they don't know I'm here. I'm defecting."

His bushy eyebrows drew together. "Defecting?"

I nodded, more sure with each passing minute. "Leaving my country. Stepping away from the crown. However you want to say it."

He let out a whistle. "Well, holy shit. That's gonna ruffle some feathers." Uncle Leo sounded remarkably American, but I heard a faint tinge of his royal roots in the accent he'd clearly worked to rid himself of.

I shrugged and looked back out at the ocean. "I had no choice. At my birthday dinner tonight I was to announce my marriage to Fiona Bettencourt, a lovely woman I have no intention of marrying just to make my parents happy."

Uncle Leo sat with that for a solid five minutes. "I'm willing to help you, son, but you better get a life together quick before they release the hounds to drag you back."

I twisted in my seat. "Speaking of that, can I stay with you for a bit?"

Uncle Leo closed his eyes for a second. "Normally I'd say yes, being family and all, but I just can't. They'll be pounding down my door the second they see you're gone. I'm not exactly the crown's favorite relative."

Well, fuck. There went my plan. I had been sure Uncle Leo would let me stay with him while I figured out what to do with my new life. I'd been stockpiling cash so I wouldn't have to use the royal credit cards they were sure to cut off, but I'd blow through it fast if I had to stay at a hotel.

"But I do know of a little place you could hunker down," he said finally.

"Here in North Carolina?"

He dipped his head. "Yup. The fine town of Sailfish Banks, to be exact. Got a little plot of land out there I haven't done anything with. It's yours if you're game."

Things were looking up. "I'm game."

We bounced over a curb as Uncle Leo pulled into a parking lot, mostly deserted at this time of night. A large, ugly building lay ahead, garish lights streaming from the mechanical front door. Trash blew by in the breeze. "Not gonna lie to you though, son. The land is in rough shape. The apartment over the main building might even be infested with vermin. Not sure you're up for that."

I steeled my spine. This was exactly what I'd been looking for in America. Well, not vermin. The chance to be my own person. To make a difference in a way that mattered. I'd started countless foundations in Mardelvia, only to be told by my parents that I couldn't actively run them. It "wouldn't look becoming" of a prince to actually get his hands dirty.

"Sounds like what I need, Uncle."

He threw the truck in park, tilting his head toward the building. "You need jeans."

Chapter Two
MAXINE

Into each life a little rain must fall.

That's what Mama always said, anyway. Of course in my case, it seemed like I often got something closer to a hurricane. Today, specifically, it was iced tea. And the amount of tea that Harold Schultz slopped onto the yellow cotton top of my waitress uniform qualified as more than a little.

"Oh, darlin'," the big man said, his enormous form perched comically on a tiny stool at the counter in the diner where I worked, "I'm so sorry about that." He held out a wad of napkins that would do almost nothing to save me from winning my very own wet T-shirt contest right there in the center of the Beachside Bacon diner.

"That's gonna leave a stain, Max," Franny joked, a little sympathetic smile lifting one side of her mouth. Granny was my best friend, and she was well acquainted with Harold's legendary clumsiness.

"Think it might," I agreed, holding my soaked top away from my sizable front side. "Do we have a spare in the back?" I asked Franny, coming around the end of the counter to the prep area in front of the kitchen.

"I don't think there's anything back there in size hourglass bombshell, sorry." She shrugged her narrow shoulders and returned to wiping down the counter. Sweet tea wasn't just covering me, Harold had managed to coat most surfaces inside the diner too.

"Sorry Max," Harold said again, sounding miserable.

I plated up a piece of coconut cream pie and slid it in front of him. "Don't you think about it again. I needed to run over to Walmart today anyway to pick up a few things for that kid of mine. He's determined to grow an inch every single day, I swear to you."

My shirt was beginning to feel clammy and cold in the air conditioned diner. I had six more hours to go in my shift, but knew I could squeeze a quick shirt run into my dinner break. "Am I good to run over there real quick right now?" I asked Franny.

She stopped mopping up long enough to laugh at me holding the front of my shirt away from my body. "Sure," she said. "I've got things here, just try to get back before the late rush hits."

"Sure thing," I agreed, sweeping my purse from the shelf below the register and swinging it over my shoulder. I held it in front of me as I crossed the parking lot outside, digging my keys out as I went. The nighttime air in Sailfish Banks was sticky and hot–a welcome relief from the relentless cool of the diner.

I called Bo on the way to Walmart, making sure that son of mine was doing what he was supposed to be doing at this time of night. Namely, nothing.

"I'm practicing my hymns, Mom. And right after that I'm going to knit some blankets for the elderly."

"Very funny." I could see that he was at home on the app we used to keep track of one another. It was just the two of us in the world, and maybe we were a little co-dependent that way, but he said he didn't mind it, and it made me feel warm and fuzzy somehow, having Bo keeping tabs on me.

"Homework done, just watching a show."

"Gator's not over, is he?" Bo's friends were mostly good kids, but there were one or two of them who I didn't trust as far as I could toss them, and Gator was number one on that list. He didn't mean to get into so much trouble, I didn't think. He just didn't have any real adult supervision in his life. Though actually, if I was Bo's adult supervision, it was a wonder he'd made it to seventeen with relatively few scrapes along the way.

"Nah, he had something he had to do for his sister. I'm on my own tonight."

"Okay good." I pulled into the parking lot in front of Walmart and idled for a moment as we finished talking. "Well, I'm stopping in at Walmart real quick. I'll grab you a couple more T-shirts? Do you need socks? Panties?"

"Please don't refer to my underwear that way," he groaned.

My heart lifted inside my wet, sticky chest. I loved that Bo and I had this kind of relationship, where I could still tease him about things like underwear. I guessed that was the result of almost eighteen years of nobody but him and me. "Do you need any?"

"Yeah, maybe a couple pairs. Get the laciest ones you can find, okay?"

"Super sexy. You got it."

"See you later, Mom."

"Love you, baby." I hung up and scanned the parking lot before hopping out of my truck. Sailfish Banks was as safe as they came, but it never hurt to be careful. We got a lot of out of towners this time of year, and while they mostly stuck to the newer, shinier part of town, I hadn't gotten this far on my own by being careless.

The air conditioning inside Walmart was blasting and I shivered as I hugged my arms over my chest, collecting stuff for Bo and a simple yellow T-shirt for myself as I headed to the dressing rooms in the back. You'd think a woman could buy a T-shirt without trying it on, but sometimes the girls challenged even the most generous-looking garments. And I was desperate to get into something dry.

In the dressing room, I pulled off the soaked shirt, wishing I'd thought to grab a box of wet wipes on my way back. I was just going to be sticky–there wasn't much I could do about that. But I didn't want to pull on a new shirt while I was still damp.

I glanced around the little space, not finding a ton of available towels hanging helpfully next to signs inviting me to sop up the tea still dripping down my back. There was the curtain, however. And I was out of options.

I grabbed both sides and backed into the curtain, pulling it against my back and wiggling side to side to try to sop up the remains of Harold's sweet tea.

"You've probably never even been inside a dressing room," a male voice suggested loudly from the entrance to my left. "Just go in there and make sure those fit."

"All right," said a second voice, distinctly male, and with an accent I couldn't quite place.

I'd rotated slightly and was successfully mopping up my front, when the curtain was yanked from my hands. "Hey!" I cried, as the now-open curtain revealed the culprit and a whole lot more of my top half than I was used to showing off to strangers.

"Oh," the man said, his eyes dropping to my assets and then leaping back to my face as his handsome face turned a deep shade of crimson. "Madame, please accept my sincerest apologies," he said, the accent pronounced now as he dropped everything in his arms except a single pair of blue jeans which he now lifted between us, draping one leg over each of my shoulders and then stepping back and averting his eyes.

For a moment, I had no words. And that was pretty rare for me. But embarrassment was doing a fancy little tango with anger inside my chest, and some other part of me was admiring the general appearance of the man who'd just draped me with a blue-jean apron.

"What the hell are you doing in the ladies' dressing room?" I asked him, gripping the pant legs tightly over my chest.

His blush had not subsided, and he bent low to pick up all the items he'd dropped. "I didn't realize," he said, standing back up. "I'm so sorry, I've never done this before." His eyes, when they touched mine briefly and then shot away, revealed themselves to be a deep shade of blue I wasn't sure I'd seen before. Like an ocean with fathomless depths. And his jaw was squared and strong, covered with a dark stubble.

"You've never barged in on a woman changing her shirt before?" Part of me was still angry, while part of me just wanted to hear that accent one more time. At least the jeans were nice and dry.

"No," he said, the blush finally beginning to subside. "I, ah... madame," he said, finally meeting my gaze and holding it.

I did not like being called "madame" one little bit. "I'm not seventy-five," I pointed out.

"Of course not. No, a seventy-five year old woman would not look... er, no, that isn't what I meant to say at all."

"I'm not giving you these pants back," I told him.

"No," he said, seeming to agree this was a wise plan. "I will just..." he began backing out of the doorway, back to the central area where he'd made a wrong turn in the first place. "I apologize again," he said, finally turning and leaving me there, draped in denim.

I let the curtain fall back in place, wiped myself down with his jeans, and put back on my bra–a little damper than I'd like– and finally, the T-shirt.

I felt oddly violated, though clearly it had been a mistake. Still, who wanders into the ladies' dressing room and goes ripping open curtains? And where in the world was that accent from?

It didn't matter. And the fact there was a very handsome stranger with a fancy accent roaming around Sailfish Banks didn't matter either. I needed to get back to work.

I gathered up my stuff and headed for the registers to check out, handing the cashier the tag for the shirt I wore and calming myself as she checked out Bo's stuff.

"Bad things come in threes," Mama's voice chimed inside my head. She'd had all the sayings, none of them particularly helpful. And now she'd got me worried that what had turned into a pretty crappy day was possibly destined to get worse.

"There you are," Franny called as I stepped back inside Beachside Bacon. "Feel better?"

"Not really," I told her, stashing my stuff again and tying on a dry apron. "Some guy ripped open my dressing room curtain when I was changing."

"You're kidding," she said.

"Not even a little."

"We get the weirdest tourists in this part of town," she said.

Just as she walked away, shaking her head, the chime on the door sounded and a pair of men stepped inside. One of them was familiar. I'd been serving Leo Barclay as long as I'd been working here. He and his family were well known around these parts for lots of things, not the least of which was the fact he had three very handsome, very eligible sons—not that they were in the market for women who'd been single moms since the age of eighteen. But it wasn't Leo that had me worried as he stepped in and gave me an open smile.

It was the man at his side. The dressing room invader.

And the man who'd violated my personal space was even better looking when I was fully dressed and could appreciate him properly. Tall, broad, with some kind of refined air about him that you just didn't see down here on the outer banks of North Carolina. Maybe it was that thick, dark hair pushed back from his face.

"We meet again," he said, the accent less pronounced.

"Hmph," I responded. "Seems like Mama was right." I steeled myself, since it seemed that the third bad thing had just arrived.

Chapter Three
CAVANAUGH

I knew living in America was going to be an experience, but I hadn't quite pictured my first day including a pair of breasts that had me like a deer in headlights. I was a prince. A forty-year-old single prince who'd seen scores of breasts over the years. Not to sound like an asshole, but I was not breast-averse by any means. I loved breasts. Loved admiring them, touching them, and...well, everything to do with breasts. But I'd never seen a pair like the ones on our waitress.

"You know what you want, Leo honey?" she drawled to my uncle, seeming to ignore me on purpose.

Which was fine. I wanted to remain anonymous here, it was just different than I was used to. Normally, I was stared at or pointed at in public, right before someone snapped a picture on their cell phone. For the first time since I'd been in America to visit my uncle as a teen, I was able to sit back and be the one to stare.

And this woman was beautiful. Her hair was a golden brown,

streaked with the kind of blond women in my country paid damn good money to get. Hers looked like it was natural. It was also barely contained in a sloppy ponytail, trailing down her back in soft waves. Her yellow shirt was unremarkable, but I knew that cotton was shielding the finest breasts on the continent. I forced myself to look at the menu and not her breasts. Surely I'd gained enough maturity in forty years to control my eyeballs.

"How about the OOT?"

I lifted my head to see her pointing at me with her pen, but talking to my uncle. Her blue-green eyes were framed by thick lashes.

"The what?"

She rolled her eyes and my instant reaction was to snap at her for her poor manners. No one rolled their eyes at me at the palace.

"Out o' townie, or OOT." She ran her gaze down my torso before coming back to my face. "You're clearly not from around here."

I gritted my teeth and reminded myself that I'd chosen to come here without the title and without all the privileges that came with it. "Pancakes and bacon."

She huffed but wrote it down on her little pad of paper. "Figures." She turned to my uncle, blessing him with a wide grin and a pat on the shoulder. "Be right back with some drinks, hun."

My uncle nodded and waited until she'd walked away to open his mouth. I did not mean to notice how her hips swung seductively as she squeaked across the linoleum floor, but it was hard not to notice. It was downright mesmerizing.

"I know you're not used to how things are done around here, but you'll catch more flies with honey than vinegar, Cav."

My gaze came back to my uncle's. He had a knowing look in his eye that I didn't like. "I'm not trying to catch flies."

"Could have fooled me." His lips twisted in a grin, but I couldn't respond since the waitress was returning with two plastic cups of ice water.

"Here ya' go. Food'll be up in a jiffy."

"Thank you," I said loudly, mostly for my uncle's benefit.

The woman eyed me strangely and walked away, shaking her head.

Uncle Leo burst out laughing.

"What?"

He took a sip of water. "This is gonna be interesting."

We managed to eat our meal without me pissing off the waitress again. I was fairly certain she hadn't spit in my food. Mostly because I kept an eye on her the whole time she was serving a few other tables that had filled up. She was unlike any other woman I'd met. She laughed so loud with the old guy at the counter the sound bounced off the walls of the diner. Her clothes didn't match and her nail polish had started to chip off. When she came to check on us, she kept her focus on my uncle, clearly indicating she didn't care if the food was to my satisfaction, only his.

Uncle Leo picked up the bill, with a grumbled happy birthday that was a stark contrast to the countrywide celebration that had been originally planned for this day. I felt a pang of guilt for leaving the way I did, but knew it was the only way. We climbed out of the booth when we were done eating and Uncle Leo clapped me on the shoulder.

"I think you should take a few days on the property I was talking about and then decide if this is where you want to be. It's different here."

"I want different, Uncle."

He studied me for a few moments. "Sometimes we think that, but the reality of it is too much. You've got grit, but maybe not in the ways you need for this kind of life. Come on. Let's head to the property. Sooner you face facts, the sooner you can make a solid decision."

The bell rang out as I held the door open for him, not wanting to argue so soon into my visit, but my mind was made up already. I wasn't going back. I'd turned my back on the crown for good. Whatever grit he was speaking of, I had it. I was certain.

Uncle Leo exited the restaurant and walked back to the truck. I paused in the doorway to look at the waitress, who was taking an order at a table in the corner. Our gazes locked and I felt a shot of satisfaction, knowing she'd finally been watching me.

"Thank you for everything," I called out, trying yet again to follow my uncle's advice. Wasn't the first time I'd been told I was kind of an asshole. Emilio had told me pretty much every day, but I was willing to try new things. That's what this whole plan was about.

It wasn't until I saw the blush staining the waitress's cheeks that I realized how she'd taken my comment. She rolled her eyes and turned back to the customers at her table.

I shook my head and followed after my uncle. Too bad nature had paired the prettiest pair of tits with such a prickly personality. I wasn't thanking her for the flashing, though I probably could have. That had been a pleasant surprise indeed. But now it was time to put her–and her breasts–out of my mind and get started on my new life.

We drove through a nicer part of town that Uncle Leo informed me was downtown Sailfish Banks. The shops were dark at this time of night, but the place looked like one of those sleepy beach towns in the daytime romance movies my maid watched every afternoon when she thought I wasn't looking. The light poles were lit with a soft yellow light that highlighted the mature trees and clean sidewalks.

Then we took a turn at the water's edge and went north. The shops got farther apart and the trash along the sides of the road increased again. Uncle Leo finally pulled into a small parking lot in front of a two-story building with a wood shake exterior. Not a single light illuminated the place. He angled the truck so that his headlights lit the way. Sadly, there wasn't much to see beyond the single building. Just a huge dirt lot with a dilapidated truck parked on one side and weeds growing around it.

When he turned off the engine, he twisted in my direction. "I'm going to lay it out straight for you. This place has been abandoned for years, but the way the town's growing, this could become part of the revitalization one day. Not even sure if it's sound to enter, but there's an apartment over the main building. The zoning is mixed-use so you can start a business or choose to just live here. It's all yours if you want it. I'll get the paperwork set up next week if you choose to stay."

"I'm staying," I said firmly.

Uncle Leo held up his hand. "I know you say that now. I said the same thing when I left Mardelvia too. I had my head in the clouds and more hope than sense. I didn't realize that I'd come to rely on all the privileges of being in the royal family. Out here it's every man for himself and you're coming in with a disadvantage. You don't know anyone and you have no real skills. I can only help you so much. You have to do this on your own. I tell my kids all the time they aren't getting one goddamn penny of the fortune I've accumulated with my blood, sweat, and tears. They gotta earn it and so do you."

I gazed out at the dilapidated building. The thing was hideous. An eyesore and in need of so many repairs it might be better to tear it down and start over. I should have been nervous. I should have called Emilio and gone right back to the life that was laid out for me, complete with plenty of money, assistants, and exotic vacations at all the nicest resorts across the world. It would have been the easy thing to do. But as I stared at that eyesore, I felt something growing in me for the first time that I couldn't ignore: a sense of pride.

Uncle Leo was right. I had no discernible skills other than matching the right family crown to the proper suit. Here was my chance to do something on my own. Here was my chance to test myself and see what I was capable of. Here was the opportunity to be Cav Barclay, not Prince Cavanaugh Michael Barclay of Mardelvia, second in line to the throne.

I took the keys from Uncle Leo's hand with a solemn nod. "I'll call you next week and we can get started on that paperwork."

He studied me and then nodded. "Alright then. Let's get your bags."

I got the bags out of his truck, dumped them on the doorstep of the building, and waved as he pulled away. Something skittered across the dirt and fallen leaves to my left, but I studiously ignored it. Unless it was an alligator, which was definitely a possibility out here in the Outer Banks according to the minimal research I'd done, I didn't have time to deal with it. I needed to check out my new home and figure out what I could do with the place to earn some money.

The door popped open with a loud creak. The overpowering smell of must and disuse hit me in the face. I clicked on the flashlight Uncle Leo had handed me and bounced the light around the interior. A few critters skittered across the floor and disappeared into the shadowed corners. Probably just lizards, miniature-looking gators that were harmless. I rapped my knuckles against the wall and the place didn't collapse, which I took as a good sign. Stepping farther into the building, I closed the door behind me, dropped the bags inside, and wondered what the hell I'd gotten myself into.

Even my "roughing it" days as a prince had included a hunting cabin a thousand times nicer than this place. I had no real construction skills, but I could read a menu in five different languages. I had yet to have a job working for someone else, but I had years of experience sitting on executive-level boards. I didn't know where my next meal was coming from, but I had a burning desire to succeed at keeping my belly and my soul full.

Something shiny in the middle of the downstairs space caught my attention. I shone the light on it and crept forward. My bark of laughter felt at odds with the dark nature of this dreary place. There, on the floor, covered in a thick layer of dust, was a half drunk bottle of Barclay Brandy, the official brandy of Mardelvia.

I left it there and turned in a circle, thoughts swirling in my brain. My great, great, great—maybe a few more greats—grandfather had started the brandy company. Everything the Barclays touched turned to gold and so did his brandy. I'd left the royal family in Mardelvia, but maybe my days of having the very best spirits money could buy had given me a skill that could transfer to this backwoods town on the edge of the Atlantic ocean.

Suddenly exhausted, I cleared a spot of dust with my foot, dropped to the floor and stretched out, laying my head on the softest of the two duffle bags. Digging in the other, I found the burner phone I'd brought with me, fired it up, and immediately called the number Uncle Leo had scratched on the torn napkin from the diner. Of course, it went straight to voicemail, but I left a very kind message—dripping in honey, not vinegar—and hung up, hoping they'd call me back first thing tomorrow morning.

I finally had a decent idea and I needed a contractor to help me.

Chapter Four
MAXINE

While most people looked forward to Friday, I adored Wednesdays. I had every Wednesday off, for one thing—though I honestly didn't mind my job one little bit, especially since it was a big part of keeping my little family safe and fed. No, Wednesdays were my favorite because they were a happy mid-point to the week. I used them to assess what had happened so far and see if there was anything I needed to shift for the rest of my week.

"I like this one." Bo interrupted my Wednesday morning meditation, appearing in the living room holding a bright pink Post-It in his hand and wearing a grin that told me he was teasing me.

I sighed, rising from the soft square pillow I kept under the window. Meditation was something new. And it turned out I wasn't very good at it. But that would change. I had at least four sticky notes in sight of that pillow assuring me that I was making progress and to give myself time and space.

"Maybe you could learn from it," I suggested, following my

son into the kitchen. When had he gotten so much bigger than me? His shoulders were so broad. My son was practically a man and it was equal parts terrifying and wonderful.

"Let's see," Bo said, leaning against the counter and peering at me over the note. "'*You are a good mother and your son is a delightful young man.*'" He chuckled, and then pulled the note to his chest. "Aw, Mom. You find me delightful?"

I snatched the note from his hand. "It's an affirmation, Bo. It's something I'm working to make true."

His jaw dropped comically. "You think I'm *not* delightful?"

I swatted his too-big bicep. "You're just a kid. But there's hope." My heart swelled inside me as he laughed, and I didn't bother trying to restrain the giggle that tumbled out of me in response. Bo was my person. It had been just the two of us since the day he was born, and every bit of my time and energy had gone into trying to make him the very best man I could. It was a tall order, considering I didn't have any great examples to work with.

"Well, I hope you manage to make this one real," Bo said, sticking the note to the counter. "It's super important."

I paused, turning to face him as I reached for the handle of the refrigerator. "It is, Bo. It's my number one goal in life. To see you happy and successful. I hope you know that." I watched the easy grin slide from his handsome face to be replaced by a tender look.

His eyes shone as he stepped closer to me and wrapped those big arms around me. Where had my tiny little boy gone? "I know, Mom. And you're already a great mother. I'll get to work on being more delightful."

I hugged my son, trying to appreciate the moment, to be

present and aware that just like all those little-boy days I let slide right by me, this one would be gone soon too.

I will not cry. I will not cry.

Bo released me, and we moved in quiet synchronicity around the kitchen as I poured myself a cup of coffee and sat at the little two-person table pushed against the wall. We didn't have a lot of space, but it had always been enough for us, and even though I didn't live in the fancy part of town, this little corner of Sailfish Banks was safe and quiet. We had a good life, something confirmed by the sticky note pressed to the wall next to the table that read: *I have a good life.*

My son slid into the seat across from me with a bowl of cereal and a comically enormous glass of milk. "So," he said, drawing out the word.

Every pulse of my Momdar switched on.

"What?" I asked, knowing something was up just by the way he'd said that word.

"It's not a big deal," he suggested, following this announcement with an enormous spoonful of cereal that required me to wait for the rest.

My mind spun. What was it this time? Had he been suspended for fighting again? Bo didn't get along with a couple of the kids from the other side of town. Or had he said something he shouldn't have to the sheriff's wife? She'd made a few remarks about me in Bo's hearing and he'd taken issue with her words. That had not been a good day. Picking your kid up at the local jail was never fun.

But Bo was a good kid. I knew he was, and he was all I had.

I steeled myself with a deep breath and let my eyes linger for a moment on a sticky note pressed to the wall next to the other: *We can handle whatever comes our way.*

"Don't freak out."

I'd considered writing that one on a note, but I tried to keep things positive. "You better go ahead and tell me because I'm getting close. You know I hate suspense."

"So you know my friend Gator?"

I did. I did not especially like a lot of Bo's friends. That said, they were all good kids who just didn't have the privilege of coming from families that could devote to them the time and attention they really should have. As a result, these boys were all close to manhood and found themselves in grown-up sized bodies with not-quite grownup minds and not a lot of guidance. I tried to be sympathetic.

"Tell me, Bo."

He sighed. "So Gator and Colby and me took out Gator's dad's old boat yesterday afternoon."

"After school," I suggested.

Guilt flickered across my son's face. "We only skipped seventh period."

I rose, moving to the junk drawer to retrieve my Sharpie and a stack of green sticky notes. I wrote carefully: *I will attend all my classes because my future is important.* I peeled off the note and stuck it to Bo's hand.

"Well this will solve all my problems," he said, one side of his mouth lifting in a smirk.

"The power of our thoughts is real, Bo. And affirmations remind us who we want to be."

"Right."

"So what happened with the boat?" I asked, a small part of

the joy I'd been feeling that morning draining away. It was amazing how much control over my feelings my son had. I reminded myself to write another affirmation later: *I am in control of how I feel.*

"We headed south to grab some snacks from the pier store by Wander Cove, and Tony Russo and his buddies were all out there in that stupid cigarette boat he's got."

I nodded, picturing the rich kids in their shiny fast boat. Trouble.

"So we pulled up and got snacks. I swear we ignored them, Mom, just like you always say to do."

"Good. But you're telling me a story, so I'm guessing we've got more coming." I braced myself for the inevitably dark moment. All stories had them.

"Yeah. So they followed us when we took off, and they were being really obnoxious, yelling things and generally being fuckwads."

"Language," I said, fatigue swamping me as a wash of hopelessness flooded my veins. Was this how life would always be in Sailfish Banks? Constant class warfare for no reason at all? It had been that way when I'd been in school, and it seemed nothing had changed. The haves were rich and unfeeling, and the have-nots did the best they could with nothing, always at the mercy of the jerks who lived on the south end of the island. I sighed. "Just tell me the bad part."

"Gator had a flare gun in the boat, and he shot it at them."

Fury and fear replaced the exhaustion and I sat bolt upright. "Bo Samuel Waddell, you better tell me right now that no one was hurt and those shiny rich boys got home safe to their mamas."

"It was more the boat..."

Dollar signs flashed before my eyes. "Son..."

"They're coming after Gator to pay for the paint job."

"Gator's family can't afford that."

"Just wanted to tell you in case you heard it somewhere else. I was there, but I didn't do anything, I swear."

I nodded. "That's the real issue, isn't it?"

Bo stared at me, and I focused on the face of near-adult in front of me, forcing my mind to stop replacing it with the round rosy-cheeked baby I'd raised for the last two decades of my life. Coddling him wouldn't make him strong and good. "Mom..."

"You're going to help Gator pay for that damage. You could have stopped him, couldn't you?"

Bo dropped my eyes and I saw the acknowledgment of his complicity hit him. "Yeah."

"I know it's hard, son. But you can be the one who keeps those other boys straight. You can be for them all the things their families aren't." I reached for his big hand, dropping mine on top of it and giving it a squeeze.

"I'll ask for some extra hours at the marina."

"Good boy."

"Mom?"

"Yeah?"

"I'm really sorry to cause trouble for you." He was. I knew he was. Bo had always had a deep understanding of the complex social sphere that operated in the beautiful and strange place where we lived. He knew I struggled too.

"It's okay, son. This is how we learn."

He turned his hand over and squeezed mine back, and his

eyes softened as he looked at me. "You're a good mom," he said, sending my poor heart skittering around inside me.

How were parents supposed to survive the sheer volume of emotion that raising kids inspired? Maybe having Bo at eighteen and on my own had been hard, but I wouldn't trade a single second of the time I'd gotten with this kid.

The sheer force of love threatened to overwhelm me as he rose and took his bowl to the sink. "I better get to school. I've heard that I should attend all my classes because my future is important."

"Go to school," I agreed.

Bo kissed my cheek and headed for the back door, turning around as my phone rang on the counter. "Grab it for you?"

I held my hand out, and Bo picked up my phone and placed it in my palm. "Love you Mom. See you later."

"Love you, buddy."

The call was Cyrus Mole, one of the local contractors my daddy had worked with before he died. I hit the speaker button and put the phone on the table, picking up my mug as I said, "Morning, Cyrus. What's going on?"

"Hey Max, how're things?"

"Sunshine and roses like always."

"Well, that's good to hear. Same over here."

"Glad to hear it. Can I help you with something?" Cyrus called when he had a job, which was usually good news for me. I still had all Daddy's old connections around the local building and fixing realm, and I liked helping the guys connect when I could. For a small fee, of course.

"Wondered if you have a few minutes this morning to meet

me at the old Daniels Donuts? Sounds like Leo's finally gonna do something with the place."

"Yeah, I can do that. What time?" That was good news. Daniels Donuts had sat vacant for more than twenty years, the old shop and apartment above it slowly becoming more and more dilapidated as the lot around it became home base for feral cats, homeless folks, and teenagers who were up to no good. It'd be great to see that land used for something that would improve this end of Sailfish Banks. I'd heard Leo Barclay had bought it a few years back, but so far hadn't seemed motivated to do much with it.

"Ten?"

"I'll see you there," I told him.

Just over an hour later, I pulled up in front of the dark shop, which at this point didn't have a sign of any kind, and was plagued by peeling paint, missing windows, mildew, and trash scattered around outside.

I didn't see Cyrus's truck, but figured I could get eyes on the place and get some idea of what he might be thinking. I grabbed my pink notebook and my favorite feathered pen, and stepped out of my car, breathing in the hot salty air of midmorning in the Outer Banks.

The place was a mess, that was for sure. I walked around the building once, noting the out of code electrical panel on the back, the crumbling concrete. When I got back to the front, Cyrus still hadn't appeared, so I climbed the creaky steps to the front door and tried the knob.

The door swung inward with a sharp crack, and for a moment I thought I'd taken it right off its hinges. Relief swept through me when the thing stayed attached, but it was replaced quickly by fear and then by irritation as I noted a hulking form standing in the middle of the vacant space.

"Hello, Madam. Can I help you with something?"

It was him. The overly handsome out of towner from the diner. Things clicked into place as I remembered that he'd been with Leo, and this was Leo's place... His fancy clothes were crumpled and smeared with dust, and there was a surprising amount of growth along his jawline compared to the previous day. The most irritating thing–besides being referred to yet again as "madam"--was that he was still ridiculously handsome.

"I'm meeting Cyrus Mole here," I said, drawing myself as tall as I could manage. It was tough. I was only about five feet on a good day.

"For what purpose, might I ask?" the stuffy hot guy asked me.

I frowned at him. "Not sure that's your business," I told him. Maybe more snarky than intended, but man, this guy bugged me. "Why are you here?"

"I am also meeting Cyrus Mole this morning."

I looked him up and down, then noted the two enormous duffle bags pushed to one wall at the side of the space. "Did you, ah... sleep here?" Maybe my initial assessment had been off. Was this guy down on his luck? Strangest tourist I'd ever encountered...

The man sighed as if I was just too tedious to answer. "If you must know, I did, yes. Which is why I'm meeting with Cyrus. I need to return this establishment to some kind of working order and create a proper living space above it. My uncle assured me that Cyrus could help me with that."

Cyrus could, I knew. But only with my help. I sighed. "Why

don't you start by showing me around?" I suggested. "And then when Cyrus gets here, I'll have a good sense of what we're going to need."

The man's jaw dropped open slightly and then he regained himself, snapping it shut and narrowing his eyes slightly at me. "Forgive me, madam, but I don't really see why it would behoove me to give the waitress from the local diner a tour of this dangerous building. I'd never forgive myself if you were to be hurt. And there are... vermin." His nose wrinkled as he confessed this last part, and I had to stifle a laugh.

"Yeah, you don't seem like the type to do well with vermin." I imagined him huddled in a corner the night before as the local wildlife who'd no doubt claimed this place scuttled around. This was certainly the most pompous homeless man I'd ever encountered, that was sure. At least he wasn't staring at my chest this morning.

I stepped away from the frustrating man in the center of the shop and let my eyes wander the place, assessing as they went. "You gonna do donuts?"

When no answer came, I looked back at the man, taking in his look of utter confusion. "Am I...?"

"This was a donut shop. Daniels Donuts."

He tilted his head to one side. "No, I don't think I'd be very good at that. I don't know what a donut should taste like."

It was my turn for confusion. "You've never had a donut?"

He shook his head lightly, a tiny smile lifting one side of the sculpted lips. Damn, he was handsome. How could a man who'd slept in a cockroach-infested, abandoned building without running water possibly look this good? "They don't make donuts in Mar... uh, where I grew up, I'm afraid."

"Where'd you grow up?"

That question shut the guy right down, and before I could dig any deeper, the door crashed open again, and Cyrus's rotund form stepped into the little space, clad in a "Doin' Deeds in the Sand" shirt and a pair of floral swim trunks.

"Hey Cyrus, what's up?" I asked him. "Got here a couple minutes early, and, uh..." I indicated the man in the rumpled pants, waiting for him to supply a name, but he did not. "This guy here showed me around a bit."

"Yes, hello," the man crossed the space and offered Cyrus his hand. "I'm glad you're here. I'd like to discuss refurbishing this establishment and creating a sensible living space above. I think we'll need to do a bit of expansion, and there's plenty of land, so I'd like to talk about outbuildings, perhaps. Maybe you could help me understand the local environment, suggest what sort of business would flourish here?"

Wow. That was the most words I'd heard Fancy Pants speak at once. And that accent... if he wasn't grumpy and irritating, it could potentially have some panty-melting qualities.

But I didn't trust men as a general rule, and especially not condescending ones with stuffy accents and very square jaws. Whatever this guy was here for, I was going to stay far away.

After making a decent referral fee for setting up his project, of course.

Chapter Five
CAVANAUGH

Cyrus scratched the few remaining hairs on his head. "Well, I can't say what's the best business, but I do know this here area is starting to be coveted. Everyone expects the revitalization of the town to sweep north through here. You might be looking at a sweet spot given a few years' time."

I nodded, feeling excited about this project now that the sun was up and I had someone—well, maybe two someones—who could help me bring this idea to life. "I'm thinking about building a bar with an apartment above it. Maybe some small outbuildings that could become rentals? Do people rent homes?"

The woman chuckled, staring at me like I'd grown two heads. Probably because I confessed to not knowing what a donut tasted like. I should not have said that out loud. For some reason, I'd felt the need to keep the conversation going. Her accent was like foreign music to my ears. She had that southern drawl everyone had around here, but hers sounded like every syllable ended in a musical note. She didn't like me, that much was clear, but her voice was still enjoyable.

"Do people rent homes?" Her eyes got comically large. "Like in general? Or just around here?"

This was where I should have done more homework about the area. "Uh, around here?"

"Sure, sure. Short term rentals go for a pretty penny around here, 'specially spring through summer." Cyrus nodded, looking around the space. "That should be no problem, but you're going to need to get a liquor license going as soon as possible." He walked off to examine the walls, muttering under his breath.

"You got the cash to renovate this place?" the woman asked, carefully studying me in a way that made me uncomfortable. Like she saw too much.

"That is a ridiculous question."

She stepped closer. "Is it, though? You slept here last night. I don't see a car out front." She shrugged and her tank top shifted enough to expose a line of black lace that had my eyes drifting. "I don't even know your name."

My gaze snapped to her face. "Cavanaugh Barclay, Madam."

She rolled her eyes and stuck out her hand. She'd painted her nails at some point between last night and this morning. "Maxine Waddell. And quit that madam stuff. Makes me feel ancient."

I shook her hand, surprised at the strength there. Most ladies I shook hands with just gave me the tips of their fingers and a limp shake. This woman shook like she meant it. "Maxine Waddle" I repeated back, trying to get the accent right. I'd never heard of anyone with that kind of name.

"Waddell," she snapped, accent on the second half.

"Waddle," I said again, purposely putting the accent on the first half just to see her cheeks take on that pink tinge again. I shouldn't be teasing her, but there was something glorious about being able to put her on the defensive instead of always me. Being the stranger in this country had me out of sorts, but teasing Max was making me feel right at home.

She opened her mouth to fire at me with something horribly rude, I was sure, but Cyrus beat her to it. He'd wandered back and looked at our hands, still holding each other in some sort of grip challenge. I let go of her immediately and put my hands in my pockets.

"I think Max better give this place a once over. I won't have a crew available for at least a month." Cyrus gestured to Maxine. "Maybe you and Bo can help this fellow with the demo portion?"

All that excitement of picking a business deflated. A whole month? I couldn't stay here for a month without getting started on my plan. I had to build a life here quickly so I could prove to my parents, once they found me, that this was the best path for my future.

"Oh, I don't know, Cyrus," Max was saying, looking around the place. "Bo has summer school on account of failing Spanish. He needs that to graduate, and I have the diner."

Cyrus nodded thoughtfully. "I know, I just thought maybe you'd know a few other guys who could help too. Maybe just oversee the project until I can get my crew here? And Bo might benefit from a job to keep him busy."

"Who is Bo?" I snapped, wanting to be let back into the conversation about my own property.

Max eyed me warily. "Bo is my son." She turned back to Cyrus. "You might be right."

"'Course I'm right. You forget I worked with your daddy a long time. I know that boy of yours and I know I can trust you." Cyrus turned to me. "You're in good hands with Max."

He clapped me on the shoulder and walked out, whistling under his breath and leaving me with the waitress with the bad attitude and the gorgeous breasts. Neither of which would help me get my bar and apartment going.

"I'm not sure what just happened, but I won't be needing your–"

"I'd go ahead and not finish that statement," she cut me off. She spun her finger in the air. "You clearly need help and I'm the only help you got. I'll be here at ten every morning until three when I leave for my shift at the diner. Walk the property with me and I'll make you a list of things to buy so we'll be ready tomorrow."

My jaw dropped. This was not how things were done. I gave the orders and everyone else jumped to follow them. This woman barked orders like she was born to the position, a fascinating juxtaposition with her station in life. What station, I wasn't sure. Was Max a construction worker moonlighting as a waitress? Or the other way around?

She clapped her hands and spun around to walk the first floor, phone out and thumbs flying across the screen. I quickly caught up to her and tried to read over her shoulder, but she always moved away too fast. When she kicked the wall and her tennis shoe went through the drywall, she shook her head and added to her list.

"Could you not punch holes in the walls?" I growled.

Max spun on me and I realized I was following her too close. Her fantastic breasts were almost pressed against my chest. I cleared my throat and inched back.

"I barely tapped it. These walls probably have water damage. You'll want to call some guys to have the roof replaced as soon as possible. We're entering the rainy season soon and we can't put up new drywall until the roof is finished."

My head was already spinning and I hadn't even gotten a look at her list. "How do you know all this?"

She sighed and put her hands on her hips, pulling her tank top tight. The thought of dealing with her every day in various tank tops and knowing exactly what her breasts looked like was causing a headache to bloom.

"My dad was a contractor. I grew up helping him on jobs. I know I'm just a lowly waitress, but I do know what I'm doing. All the contractors around here call me in to help coordinate projects and ask for my opinion. I won't lead you wrong."

Perhaps they did things differently here in America. Where I was from, contractors were paid considerably more than food servers. Why would she choose to be a waitress when she could do so much more with these skills she spoke of?

"Why are you not a contractor?"

Maxine rolled her eyes. I found I did not like her eye rolling. "Some of us can't afford to have a job that has highs and lows, hot shot. Waitressing is guaranteed income." Then she spun away from me and headed for the back door. She popped it open and the door knob came off in her hand. "Add that to the list," she muttered, handing it to me.

I took it and raised my gaze to the ceiling. I had a feeling that patience should be the first thing on that list of things I needed to procure.

"Oh, crap," Max muttered, pulling my gaze back to her. She was standing on the edge of the doorstep, gazing down at the ground below. I'd found the same thing early this morning. Apparently, whatever steps had been there were long gone.

Coming up behind her, I looked down. It was easily a five foot drop. "Good thing you're wearing tennis shoes."

I jumped down into the dirt and looked back up, holding up my hand to block the harsh sunlight. Max had edged away from the door. "I'll go to the front and come around through the side."

I shook my head. "I haven't walked the property yet. I'm not sure what's back there. I'd prefer if you just jumped."

Her hands came to her hips again. "And I'd prefer not to break my legs."

I dropped my chin to my chest to hide my smile. This woman's mouth and the things that came out of it were highly irritating but also quite entertaining. There was no one like her in Mardelvia. At least not around the palace. "Have a seat and I'll help you down."

Pretty sure she rolled her eyes again, but I was too busy staring at her curvy legs which were now eye level. I hadn't taken notice of them before, mainly because her breasts seemed to steal the show, but the woman was blessed with curves all over.

I smacked the door kick with my palm, irritated with myself for noticing. "Sit down."

"Jeez," she muttered, sitting down and bumping me as she did so. She smelled like Sweet Betsy, the scent of those fleeting childhood visits at my uncle's place. His whole property had been lined by those bushes, letting out a fragrance that perfumed the air. "I'm coming. You don't have to order me around, you know."

I looked her right in the eyes, the floor level putting her at my height. The irises of her eyes really were extraordinary. They were a sky blue at the moment, staring at me warily. Stepping just a fraction closer, I put my arms around her and paused. She sucked in a breath and gave just the smallest dip of her head. I let my arms close around her and pulled her into my body and off the step. Her breasts had nowhere to go but to spill up between us, her hands finding my shoulders and gripping tightly there.

She was warm, a firecracker of attitude and intelligence, wrapped up in a sensual package of flesh and curves. Her eyelashes fluttered as I stepped us away from the building, the moment freezing in time. Max's cheeks went pink and I let her slide down my body until her feet hit the ground. I found that while I did not care for this woman much, I very much liked the feel of her body pressed to mine. And if I didn't let go soon, she would know exactly how much I liked it.

Max's fingers pushed away from my shoulders and then her body was gone, a cool breeze between us as we both stepped back. She tugged on the bottom hem of her tank top while I cleared my throat and looked over at the abandoned truck on the property. What was going on here? I did not have time in my master life plan to be feeling up the local waitress-turned-contractor. If I didn't get my business going before my parents found me and had me dragged back to Mardelvia, there would be only one body I'd ever be feeling up and that was Fiona's. As lovely as Fiona was, she was no curvy waitress with fire in her eyes. She was more like the little sister I never wanted.

"So, uh, where do you plan to live while we demo this place?" Max asked, also looking like she wanted to be anywhere but here with me and this ridiculous tension between us.

I shrugged. I didn't care where I slept. I just wanted to get going on this project. "Probably on the floor of what will become the bar. Or maybe in that truck." I nodded to the abandoned vehicle. Pretty sure someone had shot a hole in the side of it.

Max sighed. "I'll add a sleeping bag to the list."

Chapter Six
FIONA

"He's being a child," the queen snapped.

"He's forty," the king drawled.

I had a feeling my commentary wasn't necessary quite yet. I let the two spar with each other a bit longer before clearing my throat. The queen lifted her head and leveled her gaze at me as if just remembering I was in the room. One paid attention when the queen had one in her sights. She was a beautiful woman, who'd only gotten more fierce the older she got. I had every intention of being just like her when I grew up. But that could only happen if my wayward boyfriend got his princely arse back in the country and married me like everyone had planned since we were kids.

"You must go get him, Fiona."

My mouth went dry. That is not what I expected from the early morning summons by the king and queen. Information, perhaps, on where Cavanaugh had gone, or at the very least, a plan for his return.

"Pardon?"

The queen stood, her eyes blazing. "You heard me. Go to America and bring him back home."

I had a vision of carrying the man over my shoulder onto a plane and nearly let out a nervous giggle. "How do I go about doing that?"

The queen let out a frustrated sigh. "You're a woman, Fiona. Use your feminine wiles to tempt the boy back home. It's really not that complicated."

My feminine wiles? I was not sure I possessed the kind of wiles that would bring Cavanaugh back home. It was not a secret that he and I were close, but I was fairly certain everyone in our inner circle understood we were just friends. All the best royal marriages were made from friendship, Mother always said. I had high hopes that we might come to love each other, but apparently Cavanaugh did not feel the same way. The fact that he felt the need to disappear in the middle of the night to escape me stung just a bit.

"He's at my brother's house." The king stood and moved to the window, staring out at the extensive gardens that the Mardelvia palace was known for. "I'm sure of it. Leo was always his favorite. I should have expected this."

"Excuse me, Father." Archibald, Cavanaugh's older brother and heir to the throne, came into the room, silent footsteps on the thick carpet. He looked just like Cavanaugh except for the tight lines around his eyes that spoke of responsibility and stress. "I found Emilio. He's in the Bahamas and claims he has no idea where Cav went."

"He pulled a Leo," the queen snapped.

"Seems like he might have. The note didn't give any

specifics, but he didn't take his personal cell phone. Found it in his room behind the air conditioning grate."

"Dear God, he's gone full Leo," the queen muttered.

"That's enough," the king finally commanded, turning around to address the room. "Fiona, you will go to America and talk sense into my son. If you do not, I don't need to tell you how bad this will look for you. Archibald, let's strategize a story the press will accept."

The king swept out of the room, Archibald hot on his heels. I stood there staring at the carpet in a stupor, angry at how the king spoke to me and feeling just a bit of shame sneak in too. Cavanaugh had left because he was to announce our engagement at his birthday party. This was my fault and I needed to make it right.

A sniffle had me looking up. The queen had a tissue pressed to her mouth. Ah, the battle ax had moved into the crying stage. I moved over and leaned down to put my arms around her bony shoulders. She was a strong one, but losing one's child would be a blow for anyone.

"I shall bring him back. Do not worry," I whispered in her ear before releasing her and exiting the room displaying more confidence than I felt.

The good thing about being on an official errand for the royal family was the use of their money to get things done expediently. The private jet had me landing in North Carolina before I could formulate a precise plan of action. The black sedan and driver who met me on the tarmac were par for the course. We'd be highly conspicuous, but I never learned to drive a car so renting one was out of the question. I'd been groomed to marry a royal my whole life, a prospect I was not sad about. Cavanaugh running away had upset my life trajectory as well, sending me down a path I had zero interest in traveling. Despite my lack of a formal plan, I had no intention of leaving America without him. My life depended on it.

The place was as green as Mardelvia, maybe even moreso, but the land was wild. Waterways were everywhere, the oceanfront stretching for miles on end. Tall grasses kept the view of the ocean to just a flicker here and there.

"Welcome to Sailfish Banks, miss," the driver said kindly.

I looked around, seeing a vibrant downtown area with scantily clad young people. Ah, yes. America. Where one could wear practically nothing and not be shamed for it. My suit jacket chafed just a tiny bit more. The downtown area gave way to more spread out properties with all manner of homes on them. Some homes looked like a place a prince would vacation while others looked ready to be condemned. Sailfish Banks was an odd place of have and have nots.

"Leo Barclay's place is just ahead, across the town line into Sunset Point."

The tree-lined driveway offered a nice entrance, the green grounds surrounding the large house reminding me of Mardelvia. Perhaps more of his birthplace stayed with Leo than we thought. The front door opened when the car came to a stop. I waited for the driver to come around and open my door. My heels crunched in the gravel drive as I came to standing and smoothed down my skirt.

"May I help you?" the stooped old woman standing on the porch asked.

"I'm looking for Leo Barclay. I'm Fiona Bettencourt."

"Ah," she said, turning on her heel and entering the house.

I shook my head and scanned my surroundings. I followed her inside, finding the house quite lovely. Different from Mardelvia, but beautiful just the same. Leo had done well for himself.

"Fiona Bettencourt?" came a deep voice to my left. A man who looked remarkably like the king came striding into the foyer. "I'm surprised to see you here."

I gave him a smile and tipped my head in greeting. "I'm surprised to be here."

That brought a smile to his face. "That sounds like Caroline's doing."

I did not agree or disagree. Frankly, I needed a moment to get used to hearing someone call the queen by her first name. Not even the king did that. At least not when I was in the room.

"What can I help you with, Fiona?" Leo asked, hands on his hips.

"I'd like to speak to Cavanaugh, please."

I waited there, expecting him to comply with my request, even as the silence stretched out.

"Cav? Is something amiss?"

I blinked twice, feeling a sheen of sweat building on my skin. No one had warned me that North Carolina was quite warm in May. Leo was clearly lying. Cavanaugh did that same look of fake sympathy when I complained of my heels hurting my feet after a long ball. Perhaps he had the same soft heart as Cavanaugh under all that icy bluster.

"Come now, Leo. It's just you and me here. I just want to talk to him. Face to face. I was supposed to be marrying him, after all. Surely you can understand me needing closure."

That seemed to get to him. He hung his head and rubbed

the back of his neck. "Okay, fine. I know where he is, but if you're hoping to bring him back to Mardelvia, you might want to rethink things. He seems dead set on staying in the Carolinas."

I nodded, saying what I knew he wanted to hear. "I understand. I just wish to speak to him."

He scribbled something on a piece of paper on the table off to the side of the foyer. He walked back over and handed it to me, not letting go of it until I looked him in the eyes. "He didn't leave because of you, Fiona."

And now the blinking back of tears wasn't fake at all. "How are you so sure of that?"

He let go of the piece of paper. "Because I was in his shoes not that long ago. It had nothing to do with a woman. It had everything to do with being my own man. I have a feeling Cav has the same need."

I nodded, processing his words as I walked out of the house and into the oppressive heat. As the driver shut the door behind me and I settled into the backseat for the drive over to the address Leo had given me, I took off the suit jacket and tried to come up with something to say to Cavanaugh that would sway him.

I had a speech all rehearsed in my head when we pulled up to the property. Then I saw Cavanaugh outside, his dark boots covered in dust, sleeves rolled up his forearms, and dirt smudged across his face. A single lock of dark hair fell over his forehead. He gesticulated wildly, his face locked in an angry expression. The rehearsed speech dissolved into nothing, not because of him, though he already looked like a different Cavanaugh, but because of who he was arguing with.

A woman. Barely five feet tall and wearing cut-off jean shorts that showed off tan legs. A tank top that suited the weather but didn't restrain her breasts at all. But it was mostly the way the woman snapped back at Cavanaugh that did me in.

In the thirty years I'd known him, he and I had never had an argument.

Chapter Seven
MAXINE

"Madam," Cav said in his very condescending–and irritatingly sexy tone, "I promise you, I am perfectly capable of hoisting that big hammer into the cabinets."

I crossed my arms and blew out a breath to keep from screaming at him. "Cav," I said back, making my voice extra calm despite the dueling anger and attraction fighting for center stage in my gut. "The hole in the wall inside says otherwise. You came within inches of the window. Not to mention my head."

We'd left the sledgehammer inside after a particularly close call. Bo couldn't help on school days, which left me and Fancy Pants to start the demo, and I'd gone against my better judgment in letting this guy help at all.

"Let's grab a drink and cool off a bit," I suggested, frowning at a long black sedan pulling up at the curb. "And then we'll try again. Destruction is kind of the point, but we have to keep the bones of the building intact so we can see what's what."

"What's what." Cav was also frowning at the black car that

was now idling at the curb. There was a single lock of dark hair falling across his forehead, and some insane urge I'd been struggling with all morning kept driving me to reach up, push it back. He'd probably bite me. We hadn't exactly established an easy rapport. The introduction of power tools into the arrangement hadn't helped.

"Yes," I snapped. "What's what. Like what needs doing, and who needs doing it."

The smallest of curves appeared at the sides of his sculpted lips as his glare turned into something slightly less angry.

Wait, was he laughing now? Making fun of me?

"What?" I asked, looking between him and the car that was just sitting there.

"Your turn of phrase is charming sometimes, Ms. Waddle, that's all."

"I'm amusing you now? And it's Wad-DELL, Cava-NAW." I enjoyed mangling his name just as he insisted on ruining mine. "Are you expecting company?"

Just as we both turned back to the car, the back door swung open, and one long pantyhose-clad leg extended, one very expensive looking black pump tentatively landing on the ground. A second later, another leg–thin and long–with another shoe joined it, and finally, a woman emerged, stepping away from the car, with one hand shielding her eyes from the glaring sun.

She wore a dark pencil skirt and a light pink, long-sleeved blouse that was clinging slightly to her chest in the heat. Her dark hair was pulled back in some kind of bun or knot, or maybe it was a French twist. Whatever it was, it gave her a professional kind of look, the kind that usually told me the woman wearing it was not from this side of Sailfish Banks. And this woman? Was definitely not from Sailfish Banks at all.

"Fi?" Cav said, his eyes widening at the appearance of Miss Prim and Proper.

"Who's Fi?" I asked, feeling a strange little jealousy percolate inside me. This woman was tall and gorgeous, and put together in a sophisticated and monied way I'd never be able to achieve, even if I had been born rich.

"Hello, Cavanaugh," the woman said, picking her way carefully over the muddy expanse in front of the sidewalk and coming to stand in front of us.

Cav's voice lowered to a hoarse grumble. "What are you doing here?"

"I think you probably know exactly why I'm here."

"Father knows where I am, then."

"It wasn't a complicated deduction," she said. "You pulled a Leo."

I watched this strange interaction, questions flinging themselves through my head, one by one.

The woman's eyes scanned Cav up and down, taking in the dusty boots, the jeans that clung rather deliciously to his thighs and butt, the button-down he insisted was a "work shirt" with the sleeves rolled up his forearms. He looked pretty good. Damn good, really. And a whole lot different than the guy I'd met the day before. I wondered what she made of the change. She clearly knew him from somewhere.

"So what do you expect happens now, Fi? We hop in your car and head back home to get married?"

I felt my spine straighten at that.

"Y'all are engaged?" Why did the thought bother me? I

didn't particularly like this guy, and he'd arrived in a haze of inconvenience and irritation, messing up my carefully planned life with his utter cluelessness and high expectations.

"Not exactly," Cav said, acknowledging me for the first time since Fi had appeared.

"Fi," he said, gesturing to me. "This is Maxine Waddell. She is a local construction expert and food server who is helping me." I noted that he'd had no trouble pronouncing my name this time.

The tall slim woman extended a pretty white hand, but I lifted my own in front of me to show her the mud smudged on my palm, and the horrific state of my fingernails. It would be like breaking a law for me to touch her, and she seemed to agree, pulling her hand back as her eyes scanned my grungy paw. "A pleasure," she murmured.

"Same," I said, though it felt like a lie. I turned to Cav. "So... we done here, then? You going back to wherever you came from?"

"He is," Fi stated.

"Absolutely not," Cav said at the same time. Then he seemed to recover slightly from the surprise of seeing this woman here on the curb of his run-down property. "Fiona, I appreciate the effort. You may, however, head back to Father and assure him that this is not a sudden case of cold feet or a flighty dalliance from which I'll recover. I've chosen a new life, and at the moment, that life involves this property, this woman, and a sledgehammer."

"Not if I have anything to say about it," I muttered. I was planning to keep my head intact, no matter what else happened here today.

Fiona shook her pretty head. "I don't understand, Cavanaugh. Was it really so horrible? The thought of marrying me, serving the kingdom?"

"Kingdom?" I repeated, looking between them.

Cav paled slightly and glanced at me before stepping close to Fiona, taking her elbow and steering her back to the car. I didn't hear what else he said to her, but it ended with him putting her back into the back seat of the car, and waving as the long vehicle pulled away.

"Let's get back to that demolition," he suggested.

"Hang on a second," I said. "How about you explain a couple things first? I don't want to spend my days taking apart this property for you, only to have you change your mind and run back to your kingdom with your fiancee." I put extra emphasis on those last couple words, the insanity of it all lacing them with sarcasm.

Cav's shoulders slumped slightly, and he blew out a breath. One big hand rose to push that thick curl from his forehead, and I felt a tiny pang of envy. What did that glossy hair feel like, I wondered? Silky and smooth? I already knew it smelled divine, infused with some kind of fancy shampoo's lingering scent. I'd gotten a bit too close when we'd pulled the counter out, and now I couldn't get the memory out of my head.

"Max, do you think maybe we could take a break? I'd like to take you to tea. And explain."

"You would like to take me to tea?" I asked him, laughing. "I'm afraid we're fresh out of tea houses here in Sailfish Banks. But I would enjoy a glass of sweet tea. Not gonna lie."

"Sweet tea, then," he said, though his nose scrunched a little as if the thought of sweet tea wasn't one he liked. "Where can we get that?"

"Just about anywhere," I told him. "But I like my own best."

This seemed to make him uncomfortable, and he said nothing, watching me for a long beat.

"So we can go to my place. I need to get cleaned up and changed for work soon, anyway." The thought of leaving sledgehammers and dust behind for the day was a welcome one. And for some reason, the idea of seeing Cav sitting at my kitchen table was also exciting. Of course, showing him my house might also have the effect of sending him running back to whatever fancy origins he'd come from. And part of me hoped it would.

I was worried about what would happen if I spent much more time with him. Despite his prickly nature and generally grumpy rich-guy demeanor, there was something about him I was starting to like. A lot. It might have just been his thick dark hair and broad shoulders. But I suspected it had a lot more to do with the glimpses I'd gotten behind all that–glimpses of a man who was looking for something, who was trying to find some part of himself he might have lost or just never found in the first place.

I half-hoped he'd see my small house, figure out I had almost nothing to offer a guy used to having tea and crumpets in the afternoon, and run back home. Because wherever this man had come from, I already knew he was going to take a tiny part of me with him when he went back.

"I suppose I'll drive," I said, my gaze sweeping the overgrown property and landing on the dilapidated red truck parked–or rather, abandoned–off to one side. "You gonna get that clunker going?" I asked this as Cav followed me around the side of my Bronco to the driver's door.

I gave him a questioning look over my shoulder as he reached for the handle. "Uh, you want to drive? Not sure I'm up for that adventure after the sledgehammer incident."

"There was no incident," Cav said, pulling the door open and stepping back. "And I do not want to drive. I was just being a gentleman." He waved me into the driver's seat, closing the door behind me, and then strode around the front of my big car to the other side. As he hoisted himself up onto the scarred leather seat, self-consciousness filled me. The car was old. And it smelled. I spent half my time carting teenage boys around, and often when they were sandy and wet, other times when they were just finishing up soccer practice. There might have been some dirty cleats in there somewhere, judging by the smell.

"Sorry for the car," I said as Cav settled himself.

He glanced around as if seeing it for the first time. "Miss Waddell, it is a perfectly acceptable conveyance."

"That it is," I agreed, giggling slightly as I pulled away from the curb and turned back toward my house. "And if you like this heap of rust, you're going to love my house."

"I'm certain I will."

Oddly, it seemed like he did. We stepped out of the car into my driveway, which ran down the side of my property next to what could only be described as a cottage. My place was pink, which was my favorite part of it, and it had a grassy front yard lined with beds of flowers. A tiny front porch held two white rockers, and inside, the space sported two bedrooms, one bathroom, a teeny-tiny kitchen, and a little front room that did duty as living room, dining room, or teenage boy hangout space, depending on what was needed at any given time.

I waved Cav inside and we took turns washing up a bit in the bathroom.

I swept through the front room, scooping up socks and shoes, random soda cans and wrappers from the protein bars Bo loved but could never seem to be bothered to clean up. When Cav joined me again, I had two tall glasses of sweet tea on the table and a plate of Lorna Doones between them. Tea and biscuits, I supposed.

"This looks lovely," Cav said stiffly, waiting for me to sit before seating himself across from me. "And your home is charming, Miss Waddell."

"Do you think it might be time to call me Max?"

Cav looked slightly surprised at this suggestion. "Would that be appropriate? I barely know you."

"You're sitting in my living room, so I think it would be okay to drop the formality."

He nodded and reached for a cookie.

I took a long refreshing sip of my tea, letting the sweet, cool liquid clear the dust from my throat and the confusion from my mind. This was my house, my world. He was the intruder here, and he had some explaining to do.

"So," I said. "Why don't you tell me where you're from and how you ended up here in Sailfish Banks?"

Cav's eyes dropped to the gingham tablecloth where his fingers traced a few of the squares. I did my best not to notice the long graceful fingers or the perfectly squared off fingernails. Wherever he and Fiona were from, they must have had really excellent manicurists around every corner. I tucked my hands under my thighs and waited for him to talk.

"Yes," he said, appearing to gather himself. Then he reached for his glass and sipped his tea before his eyes went wide and he sprayed that same tea across the table top.

I managed to dodge the spray and rose to get a towel from the kitchen, shaking my head at the thought of mopping my sticky floor later that night when I got home from my shift at the diner. First though, Bo would certainly walk through it and track sticky sweet tea all over my house. I sighed, mopping up what I could and then taking my seat again, while Cav sputtered words of apology.

"It's very sweet," he said once I was seated again.

"You wouldn't expect that, would you?" I asked. "Given that it's called 'sweet' tea."

He frowned. "Of course. That does make sense." He looked around. "I'm sorry for the mess."

I waved him off, hoping he'd just get to the heart of the matter now. Instead, his gaze had latched onto the twenty or so sticky notes covering the front of the refrigerator.

"I'm strong and capable," he said.

I cringed.

"I have everything I need for success."

Oh lord, shoot me now.

"I'm a kickass soccer player and the ladies love me?"

I dropped my head into my hands. Bo had written that one. Either my belief in affirmations was really wearing off on him or he was making fun of me.

"Affirmations," I explained, not lifting my head. "Not really meant for company. I should've taken them down, but then they wouldn't stick and I'd have to redo them all."

"Noticed a few in the lavatory as well."

Oh crap. I'd forgotten about those.

"And Max?" The question in his tone and the gentle lilt of his voice made me look up at him again. "You *are* beautiful. There should really be no question of that." The deep blue eyes held a look of sincerity I couldn't shrink away from, no matter how uncomfortable the compliment was to receive.

"Thanks," I muttered. "Like I said, those are just for me, really."

He cleared his throat and reached for another cookie, and then sipped his tea carefully, as if it might reach up and slap him.

"So," I prompted, settling back and crossing one leg over the other.

Cav's eyes followed the motion of my legs before returning to my face, a slight pink tinge dotting his cheeks above the scruff of a beard beginning. Did Cav like my legs? The thought gave me a little rush.

"Yes," he said. "I do owe you a few answers, I suppose." He settled back and cleared his throat again. "The truth is..." he shifted in his seat, delaying further.

"Cav, I'm starting to think it's really awful. You probably better quit stalling and just get to it. Plus, I need to get ready for my shift soon, and unless you want to endure a whole lot more questions than the ones I've got for you, you'll want to be done with this story before Bo gets home in about twenty minutes."

"Er. Yes. Okay." He sat up straighter. "Well, I'm not originally from here, Max."

"No shit, Sherlock."

Despite his raised eyebrows, he continued. "I was born in another country, in fact. But my uncle lives here. Leo Barclay?"

I nodded. Leo was good people.

"So when I decided it was time for me to leave home, I chose to come to the place he loved. I'd visited him a few times here when I was younger, and I remembered it being beautiful and warm, and filled with good people."

"And so how long are you visiting for this time?"

"I'm not going back." This was stated almost defiantly.

"And what's the story with Fiona? Your, uh... fiancee." I stuffed a cookie in my mouth to distract us both from whatever strange expression saying those words had brought to my face. Why did the idea of him being engaged bother me so much?

"She is not my fiancee. Not in any practical terms."

I shook my head. "Need a bit more."

"Our families believed we would make a good match," he went on. "And we grew up together. So almost from the time we were conscious, we'd essentially been promised to one another. But Fiona and I..." he trailed off, his eyes scanning the whitewashed walls for a second before finding my face again. "We've always been close friends. But that's really all there is. And I didn't relish the idea of marrying a friend, and never having the opportunity to experience the real thing."

Something about the tenderness in those last words surprised me. Men didn't wax poetic about love and romance. Not around here, at least. It was charming, in a way.

"So you ran away?"

"Our families were going to push us to make the engagement official when I turned forty."

"And when was that?" I asked.

"Yesterday."

I raised a cookie in the air. "Happy birthday, Cav."

He picked up another cookie and touched it to mine. "Thanks very much, Max. And thank you for helping me get the property sorted out."

I was about to answer when the front door burst open and three enormous young men exploded into the front room, a cloud of chaos surrounding them as whatever conversation they'd been having outside accompanied them into the tiny space.

"Hey, Mom." Bo crossed the room and bent down to kiss my cheek, then stood and narrowed his eyes at Cav. "You, uh, having a date?"

Bo's friends Colby and Gator stood behind him, their expressions more interested than I liked as they watched this exchange.

"Boys," I said, addressing them all. "This is Mr. Barclay. He is Leo Barclay's nephew, and he's new in town. Bo, you and I are helping him demo the old Daniels Donut shop on Main. And Gator and Colby? I expect you'll help him out when you see him around town."

"Yes ma'am," Colby said.

Gator, who I'd never really warmed to, continued to look at Cav suspiciously. "Where you from, man?"

I waited, realizing I still didn't have an answer to that question either.

"A little island nation near the United Kingdom," Cav said.

What the what? I'd never even heard of such a place. Unless he meant Ireland. "Where—"

Cav stood abruptly. "Well, it's lovely to meet you gentlemen," he said, shaking Bo's hand. "But I should be on my way. Thank you, Max, for the excellent tea."

I raised an eyebrow. Excellent tea didn't normally end up on the floor, but whatever.

"I'll see you tomorrow morning?" I asked.

"I'll be there, ready to swing that hammer."

"We'll see about that." I told him, crossing the living room, squeezing past my son's enormous friends to let Cav out. "You okay getting home?"

He nodded, and strode down my walkway out to the sidewalk.

"Weird cat," Colby said as I stepped back inside.

"You boys be nice," I told them, feeling strangely defensive of the handsome stranger.

"We will, Mom." Bo flopped down on the sofa, pulling the video game controllers off the coffee table and handing them to his friends. "You gonna be late?"

I glanced at the clock. Yes, I was definitely going to be late.

Chapter Eight
CAVANAUGH

I'd come back from Max's with more on my mind than before I'd left. The woman drove me mad and yet I felt another layer of guilt weighing me down for lying to her. I hadn't exactly lied, but omission was the flip side of the lying coin. I was still deceiving her by not telling her where I'd come from and about my royal family. Kind of a big detail not to offer when she opened her home to me and introduced me to her son.

I threw the sleeping bag into the back of the truck bed, having swept the truck out earlier and found keys under the seat. It took some swearing and some cajoling, but I got the engine running. It backfired every time I touched the gas pedal and the floorboard was rusted through on the passenger side, but that did not bother me. At least I had transportation.

The nights here were warm and sticky, but there was also a cool ocean breeze. With half of the inside of the future bar demolished and the debris scattered across the floor, I decided I might fare better sleeping under the stars. The hoot of a nearby owl announced my arrival. I climbed up and over the side of the truck bed, collapsing down onto the sleeping bag.

My muscles were exhausted and my hands ached from that damn hammer. I had no idea how tiny Max, who barely came up to my chest, was able to keep up with all this manual labor. I'd had trainers over the years who put me through my paces, but never had I engaged in this kind of intense labor. I had a newfound appreciation for day laborers.

The buzz of cicadas finally filled in the quiet night, assured that I was there to sleep, not disturb their territory. I put a hand behind my head and tried to plump the duffle bag into a decent pillow. What the place lacked in creature comforts it made up for in the view. Stars dotted the night sky, a few winking in and out as the cloud cover moved with the breeze. In the confusion of getting the dilapidated place started and sparring with Max, I hadn't had a single moment to enjoy the fact that I was a free man. As the night sounds filled my ears and the breeze took the edge off the heat, I felt like whooping out loud in a way very unbecoming of a prince. Then again, if this all worked out, which I was determined to make happen, I wouldn't be a prince any longer.

"Heeeyaa!" I hollered out loud, chuckling to myself at the lighthearted feeling that was entirely foreign to me.

"Keep it down or I'll call the cops!" A voice called out from somewhere in the front of my property.

"Hello?" Dammit. I didn't have a way to defend myself. I was trained in hand to hand combat and fencing, but I'd left my rapier in Mardelvia and didn't particularly want to start my stay

THE SPARE AND THE SINGLE MOM

in Sailfish by getting in a fist fight with the locals. I stayed low in the truck bed, hoping whoever was out there would just move on. I turned over to glance through the cracked windshield of the truck.

An old woman with her white hair in curlers and a cane in her gnarled hand traipsed right across my land. "If you think you can squat on this land, you're sadly mistaken, buster!"

Reasonably sure I could take an old lady if I had to, I popped my head up. "I'm not squatting. I own it." Well, I would next week when Uncle Leo came by with the necessary paperwork.

I hopped over the side of the truck and kept my hands up for the woman to see I meant no harm. She had on a sleep dress that snapped down the front, her feet in slippers that I was sure would be dirty by now if the shape of my boots were any indication. She lifted her cane in the air from twenty feet away and glowered at me, eyeing me up and down.

"Who are you?"

"I'm Cav Barclay, Leo's nephew. This is my land." I dropped my hands slowly and she dropped her cane.

"Huh. I'm Edith Carmichael and I own the place next door. Leo didn't tell me he sold the land."

I wasn't aware of who lived next door either, so I didn't blame her for being curious. "Not so much sold as he gave the land to me to use. I just started demoing the place. You'll see me coming and going a lot from now on."

"Granny?" A male's voice joined the party. A dark shadow moved forward and came to stand next to Edith. In the moonlight I could tell he was over six feet tall but couldn't make out his facial features. "You know you're not supposed to leave the house without me."

"This boy over here was hootin' and hollerin' like he didn't care about my beauty sleep." Edith pointed at me with that cane of hers again.

The man looked in my direction. "Hey. I'm Vance. Sorry about Granny. I'll get her home now. Have a nice evening." Without giving me a chance to respond, he steered her back toward the parking lot while she gave him an earful. I'd have to go exploring tomorrow when the sun was out. Find out who my neighbors were so I didn't get shot for trespassing.

Climbing back in the truck, I pulled my boots off and laid back down. I had another full day of manual labor tomorrow with Max. Edith wasn't the only one who needed her beauty sleep. I slapped at something that landed on my arm and turned on my side before drifting off into a deep sleep.

"Bloody hell," I muttered for the hundredth time that morning, reaching behind me to try to scratch my back.

I'd woken up with the sun, energized and ready for a new day of demoing and building my dream. Sadly, within seconds of waking, I also realized I'd been accosted by some sort of local bug while I slept. Every bare inch of skin was covered in red welts that itched like I'd dipped myself in itching powder. Upon dressing, I'd discovered the wankers had also gotten me through my clothes.

I lifted my hand to knock on Fiona's hotel room door, but

she swung it open, looking freshly showered and coiffed, without a single bug bite.

"Are you alright, Cavanaugh? I heard you through the door." She scanned my body, eyes widening when she focused back on my face. "What is on your forehead?"

I reached up and felt a welt right in the center of my forehead. Great. "Apparently, there are biting bugs in North Carolina."

She stepped back and let me in with a shake of her head. "Another reason to come back to Mardelvia."

"Listen, Fi. We have to talk about that."

Fiona shut the door and wrinkled her pert nose. "Actually, you should shower first. You smell like the horses when they come back from a hunt."

I lifted my arm and gave myself a whiff. She was not wrong. "Do you mind waiting?"

She pointed toward the bathroom. "Not at all. I'll have some tea brought up."

The shower did feel heavenly. I'd already forgotten the luxury of hot water, sudsy soap, and a clean fluffy towel. I felt like a new man when I stepped out of the shower. My clothes were a bit wrinkled from being in my duffle bag, but at least they were mostly clean. When I stepped out, Fiona poured a cup of tea for me, no doubt without the copious amounts of sugar Americans seemed to add.

I had a seat and accepted the tea, taking a fortifying sip before addressing Fiona. Just because I did not want to marry her did not mean that I would be cruel. "We've grown up together, practically family already. If staying a royal was important to me, I would have done my duty and married you. You are a most pleasant woman and–"

Fiona clinked her tea cup on the table rather loudly, interrupting me. "Stop right there, please."

"Fiona, I do not wish to hurt you," I said sadly, putting my own teacup down.

"I know." She smiled sadly. "While you've always been a bit of a grump, you've also always been kind. But the thing is, I realized yesterday that I do not want my future husband to describe me as 'a most pleasant woman.' I want him to feel so much more than that."

I glanced down at her hands where they lay perfectly folded on her lap. She was as much a part of the royal machine as I was, bred to be the perfect lady while turning her back on everything she actually wanted.

"If that's what you want, you most certainly deserve it."

Fiona's lips wiggled in a way I'd never seen before. "I want my future husband to look at me the way you look at that Max woman. Like you might just throttle her or kiss her, never quite knowing which."

My gaze snapped up to her face. "I do not look at her that way."

Fiona shot me a sly look. "Come now, Cavanaugh. You have never lied to me before. Don't start now."

I tucked away her insinuation, determined to examine it later. Much later. "What will you do now?"

Fiona shrugged, the ruffles of her silk blouse rippling. "I can't go back to Mardelvia. As the king stated so eloquently, I will be a ruined woman. Spurned by the prince." She widened her eyes comically. "So, I shall stay here. Mind if I join you on this adventure? Purely platonically, of course."

I thought about it, and the more I tossed the idea around, the more I liked it. It would be nice to have a friend from the old country here with me, stumbling through what it was to live in America.

"You know how to use a hammer?"

Fiona scoffed. "I do not." Her face brightened. "But you are about to open a drinking establishment, aren't you? I know how to make a Bloody Mary that will have you singing my praises."

Solutions clicked into place. "Do you know how to mix any other drinks?"

Fiona put a manicured hand on her chest. "Please, Cavanaugh. I was raised to be the lady of the house, which includes preparing all manner of drink. The royals and their family friends may be rich, but they drink like fish and it's inconvenient to rely upon servants all the time."

I grinned. "I'm not quite ready for you, but you're hired."

Fiona grinned back at me. This felt right. She and I had always felt right as friends. It was everything else expected of us that felt wrong. "Excellent."

"Maybe I can get the apartment above the garage in working order before your parents cut off your credit card."

"I hope so too. I'd hate to experience the biting bugs." Fiona grimaced, staring at my forehead.

I stood up, even more excited for the future. "I better get back to renovating. Come by any time." I looked down at her heels. "Perhaps you need to stop at the Wally beforehand and pick up some clothes more suitable for this environment."

"What's the Wally?"

I held my hands aloft. "It is a magical place. You can buy anything you could ever need for very little money."

Fiona stood. "Oh, that sounds wonderful. I shall have my driver stop there after I've updated the queen on your existence."

Stress dialed back some of that enthusiasm. "She should be happy to hear her youngest lives. Maybe you can say our tea was the first step in your plan to bring me back?"

Fiona gripped my arm. "I will say what I must, but know I'm here to stay. Now go build that apartment!"

I patted her hand and left, eager to get to the construction site and get to work with Max. The truck didn't seem to want to go over forty miles per hour, but eventually I made it back home. It let out one last backfire, which got Max's attention as she stared at the exterior of the building, hands on her hips. She was in another pair of cut-off jean shorts, this time with little white strings that hung down and danced along her tan skin.

I climbed out of the truck and came over to her side. There it was. The scent of Sweet Betsy. Reaching down, I scratched at a bite just behind my knee. I felt Max look over at me before gasping.

"I know. I slept in the back of the truck with the biting bugs."

"Ah yes, the mosquitoes. You're going to get eaten alive, Cav. Text me next time before you do anything crazy and I can offer some advice." She shook her head, trying not to look at the bite on my forehead and failing. She doubled over and laughed so hard I couldn't help but smile at my own expense. It was a bit funny and I did enjoy the sound of her laughter.

"Come on. Let's go buy some netting first." She walked to her Bronco and waited for me to open the door and help her up. She looked at me out of the side of her eye and burst out laughing again.

I looked up at the clear blue sky and huffed. Starting over in a new country was harder than I thought. But Max somehow made it much better.

Chapter Nine
MAXINE

We needed to get to work, but there was no way I could let anyone get eaten alive by mosquitos on my watch. The very least I could do was to take Cav over to the Sports and Shorts and get him some decent mosquito netting.

"So they don't sell this netting at Walmart?" Cav asked on the ride back to the worksite. "They really seem to sell everything there."

"You're catching on. Walmart is a good first stop, but I knew we'd find what we needed at the sporting goods store, and you don't want to mess around. These mosquitos down here will take an arm off if you're not careful."

"Seems so," he said, scratching aggressively at his arms.

"Smear some of that stuff on when we get out of the car. It'll help the itch."

"We don't have mosquitos back home," he said, sounding thoughtful.

"Do you have alligators? Snakes? Or bears?"

Cav swallowed audibly. "Ah...no."

I parked the car in front of his building and turned to him. "Well, the alligators don't climb real well, so you'll be okay in the truck for now. But the bears..."

"Perhaps this sturdy netting will dissuade them?" There was a hopeful note in Cav's voice, and while I hadn't heard of many bear maulings down here, there were plenty of bears around. And they were curious critters. It was on the tip of my tongue to offer Cav a place to stay at my house, but then I thought better of it. The guy was clearly wealthy – or had been, at least. And his uncle was certainly well off. If he hadn't chosen to stay in a motel, there was a reason for it.

Plus, maintaining a professional distance would be impossible if Fancy Pants was sleeping at my house. There was also the small matter of my son and our lack of an extra bedroom. No, inviting the hot clueless guy to stay with us would definitely not work.

I showed Cav how to fasten the netting to the back of the cab and the sides of the truck bed so he'd be protected from biting bugs from now on.

Together, Cav and I managed to finish clearing and cleaning most of the first floor through the early part of the day. It was rough, dusty work, and there was a growing heap of refuse out in front of his future bar that we'd need to get hauled away before anyone complained about it.

"Hey in there!" A scratchy male voice called through the front door as Cav and I were headed upstairs.

Cav turned and went to the door. "Well, hello."

I stepped near and peered out to see an older man in a

wifebeater and a scruff of sparse gray hair covering his jaw and his head. "Hello, Angus."

"Well, Max. I shoulda knowed you were part of this, judging by the toilet sitting out there on the curb."

Cav turned to give me a look of confusion before facing Angus again. "I'm Cavanaugh Barclay," he said. "I'm the new owner of this property, which we are in the process of refurbishing. Can I assist you?"

"Well, yeah," Angus said. "Y'all are making a ruckus over here with all the banging and smashing."

"Angus, this is a construction site, and it's the middle of the day. Not breaking any laws, I'm afraid." I crossed my arms in front of me. Angus was a weasel at the best of times, always angling for more than he was due. I wondered what he'd thought he could get out of a dilapidated building and a somewhat clueless foreigner.

"Well, I could overlook the noise, I suppose."

"Thank you sir, I appreciate it," Cav said, stepping away as if the conversation was over.

"Not quite so fast, there, Cav-ee-naw." Angus grinned and then scratched his head, looking over at the pile of construction garbage near the curb. "Maybe we make a little trade?"

Cav blew out a breath that sounded like frustration. "A trade?"

"I'm in the market for a toilet, see?"

"Angus," I said. "Take whatever you find on the curb. Just don't make a bigger mess than is already there, okay?"

"For frees?" Angus asked, looking between us, his watery blue eyes filling with glee.

"For frees," I confirmed. If he wanted to help us reduce the amount of stuff we'd have to haul to the dump, let him at it.

"Maybe I won't report y'all then, after all."

"Most appreciated," Cav said, shooting me a questioning look.

When Angus was gone, Cav turned to me. "Are we in some kind of trouble?"

I shook my head. "No, that's just Angus. Unfortunately, he's your neighbor across the street over there. He just likes to make noise if he thinks he can get something."

"What will he do with the toilet?" Cav asked, rubbing his jaw.

"I doubt we want to know."

We spent the rest of the morning clearing loose items from the apartment upstairs. A good amount of the work had actually been done up there sometime in the past, and I had a vague recollection of hearing about a buyer for this place that hadn't worked out. They must've started the job and then changed their minds.

As we pushed the remains of a rusted old bedframe out the second-floor window, Cav caught my eye. "Max, are you hungry?"

I was. Starving, in fact. "I am, yeah."

"Maybe I could take you to lunch? As a thank you for helping me?"

I hesitated. On the one hand, I liked the idea of spending time with this man, away from the dust and demolition. On the other, I wasn't sure it was wise, mostly because I liked the idea. Historically, men had not been an area of great success in my life, and as a result, I'd done my best to move in the other direction when I felt certain parts of my mind spark to life with interest. No good came from that sort of entanglement, in my experience.

With the exception of my son, I'd never gotten anything but heartache and despair as a result of getting close to a man. And that included my father.

But Cav wasn't suggesting anything besides a sandwich, and my stomach rumbled loudly as I considered it. We did have to eat, after all.

"Sure," I said. We washed our hands and arms at the wash station I'd set up when we'd begun, doing our best to remove a layer of dust, and then Cav told me he would be driving.

I eyeballed his truck, but didn't argue as he pulled open the passenger door with a loud groan of metal. The truck rumbled to life reluctantly, and Cav navigated us down the old driveway and onto Main Street, heading into the main part of town.

"There's a great sandwich shop here," I told him, pointing in front of us.

He found a spot, and came around to the passenger side to help me out of the truck. As he reached a hand up for me, I tried not to be charmed by his ongoing gentlemanliness. But it was hard. Really hard.

Especially when he kept my hand in his just a second longer than he needed to and looked down at me with an inscrutable expression in those dark eyes as we stood close on the sidewalk.

The heat of the day wafted around us, rising from the concrete, but it didn't compare to the warmth ratcheting up in the narrow space between Cav's chest and mine. His hand was strong and hot, and I knew that the longer we stood there, the less chance I had of regaining my determination to resist whatever attraction I had to him.

"Cavanaugh?" A male voice rescued me from my failing strength, breaking the spell. Cav dropped my hand and we stepped apart and turned to find Ben Barclay standing a few feet away, lifting his aviator shades to peer at the two of us.

I'd known Ben for a while–he was Leo's son. And the man was huge.

Though Cav was certainly not a small guy, Ben towered over us both, and I was betting I could have fit two Cavs inside one Ben. It occurred to me as Cavanaugh reached a hand out graciously that they must be cousins.

"Benedict?" Cav said cautiously as they shook and I felt my eyebrows rise in surprise. Ben was Benedict? Did these guys all have super fancy names?

"You got it," Ben said. "Hi Max, nice to see you again." He shot me a smile, replacing the sunglasses and looking between us. Then the smile dropped. "Oh shit, am I supposed to like, bow? Or kiss a ring, or anything like that?" He removed the sunglasses again, frowning at his cousin.

"Of course not," Cav said quickly, an uncomfortable chuckle rolling from him. "Don't be ridiculous." He looked at me. "Ben is just making a joke."

That was weird. But I was becoming used to things being weird where Cavanaugh Barclay was concerned.

"Good to see you," Ben said. "Dad said you were in town for a bit."

Cavanaugh nodded. "You too," he said. "Miss Waddell and I were about to go inside for a sandwich. Would you like to join us?"

Ben looked up and down the sidewalk, as if there might be a reason to decline on its way towards us, but then he pushed his sunglasses to the top of his head and nodded. "Sure, if I'm not intruding."

Together, we went inside the little shop and ordered at the counter. A few moments later, the three of us were in a booth by the window, Cav sitting close at my side. Even after a morning of demolition, he managed to give off an air of refined masculinity. And he smelled good too. I wasn't sure how that was possible after sleeping in a truck and smearing himself with hydrocortisone, but there it was. The man was impeccable.

"Ben has two younger brothers and a sister," Cav told me. "All born here in America."

Ben grinned at me. "Uncle Leo ran away a long time ago, and Cav here is following in his footsteps."

That was interesting. This island country where they lived must have been a real shithole if people were that desperate to get out. Only, neither Cav or his uncle seemed particularly like the hard-scrabbling desperate types. What had been so bad back home, I wondered.

"How have things been for you?" Cav asked his cousin.

I nibbled my tuna sandwich, feeling a bit like a third wheel.

"Good, mostly," Ben said. "Dad's business keeps me busy, but I have to say, I envy what you're doing here."

"I have no idea what I'm doing here, Benedict," Cav said.

"Dad says you're building a bar?"

"That is the idea, yes. But I'm technically homeless and only managing to make progress on the objective thanks to Max, here."

I stuffed a chip in my mouth, trying not to bask in his praise.

"But you're doing your own thing, Cav. Making your own way. I'd like the chance to do that, you know?"

Cav nodded, looking at his cousin with a speculative gaze. "Would you consider coming to help?"

Ben's eyes lit up. "Help? In what way?"

Cav glanced at me, as if for approval, so I gave him a little shrug.

"For now, we're just cleaning up. But soon, construction will begin for real, and I want to get a few little outbuildings set up. As rentals. Maybe you could help with that part?"

Ben was nodding. "They sell kits."

"Kits?" I asked, curious now.

"Yes. Tiny homes and trailers, little one or two room buildings that you can trailer behind a truck if you want to move them around. Maybe you could make this into a tiny home park? That would be novel. People would love to stay in those."

"You think people would like to stay in tiny houses?" Cav sounded mystified by this idea.

"We can't all grow up in a palace, cousin."

I wasn't surprised to hear that Cav had been raised in some enormous palatial mansion, but he looked extremely uncomfortable at the mention of his family wealth.

"I'm very interested," Cav said. "If you'd like to help clean up the land, get things ready for construction with us, we'd be happy for the help. In the meantime, I'll do a bit of thinking about your teensy house proposition."

"Tiny house," I said. "It's a thing."

"Tiny houses," Cav said in a low voice, clearly mystified.

It was charming, this complete lack of awareness about some of the most common things around. If I hadn't been in better control of myself, I'd be wishing I could be the one to show him all the things he didn't know about here. But I reminded myself that this was just a job. And once we got the place cleared and Cyrus got the subs in to build, I'd make a pretty penny on referral fees, and they'd go straight into the nest egg I was saving to send Bo to college.

"Thanks for the sandwich," I told Cav. "I guess we'd better get back to work."

Ben stood when we did and shook his cousin's hand again. "I've got a hookup with some equipment," he said. "I'll get it loaded up and meet you at your place. I can start clearing up the lot within the next few days, if that sounds good."

"The sooner the better," Cav said. "Glad for the help."

"Just one thing," Ben said, his smile dropping a bit. "Don't mention this to Dad."

Cav frowned, but agreed. "Sure, Ben. Of all people, I understand the fear of disappointing one's father."

Interesting.

We got back into Cav's truck, and headed back to the site.

"Seems like things are really coming together," I said. "If you can get the land cleared, we can start on the outbuildings at the same time as we take care of the main construction."

Cav actually grinned at me, and the way his dark eyes danced made my heart flip a little inside my chest. "It's incredible," he said. "I think this is the life I was made for."

We pulled back up to the property, and I saw Bo waiting out front, sitting casually on the front steps.

"Ready for the big guns?" I asked Cav, who frowned at this expression.

"Guns?"

"Muscles," I told him. "Bo is here. We'll have the apartment upstairs cleared in no time."

The guys shook hands and greeted each other. I gave Bo a grateful smile, and we all headed upstairs.

Chapter Ten
CAVANAUGH

Max's son was handsome, his limbs still lanky with youth but already packing on muscle like that of a man. I remembered being his age and thinking I had the whole world in my hands. Anything was possible if I just wanted it badly enough, I'd never die no matter the stupid things I tried when my parents weren't around, and adults might just be the stupidest humans alive. Life in general and duty to the crown had beaten most of that enthusiasm and naivete out of me, but I was finding it again here on this plot of abandoned land in Sailfish Banks.

And I had a sneaking suspicion it had a lot to do with Max Waddell.

I followed her up to the front of the building, shaking Bo's hand and walking inside to give him a quick tour. Wasn't much to see quite yet, but I could envision it all in my head. "If you come up the back stairs, you can get to the apartment up above. It's mostly demoed but we could use some help hauling all the debris downstairs."

"Sure thing, boss." Bo pulled on some work gloves and got busy filling up a contractor bag Max had put on the list of supplies to purchase. He seemed like a hard worker, a trait I admired.

I headed back downstairs to help Max in the small bathroom in the back of the building. I found her frowning at the vanity, a large streak of dirt across her cheek.

"You know, you could save this thing. New coat of paint and it'd be decent."

I stepped into the small space and brought my hand up to her face, cupping her jaw. Her gaze flew to mine, her whole face immediately flaring red at my touch. "You have something..."

My thumb swept across her cheek, rubbing away the smudge. Her skin felt soft as silk, which shouldn't surprise me. Max was a confusing mix of contradictions. She was short and small, but wildly capable. She was open and friendly, but shied away from a man's touch. She could swing a sledgehammer like a lumberjack, but had the heady curves of a goddess.

"Thanks," she whispered on a breath that whooshed out between us.

I could have been wrong, but there seemed to be a level of heat between us that had nothing to do with the warm North Carolina summer. Chasing that heat and seeing where it led us probably wasn't the smartest move, but this trip here to America was all about taking chances. I leaned down, watching the way her eyes went wide, but she didn't move back.

"Hey, Mom, you got more bags?" Bo's voice interrupted the moment.

Max lurched back, a shaky hand touching her cheek, right where my hand had been. "Yeah. There's a whole box by the front door." Her voice sounded strained and I felt a momentary twinge of guilt. Making out with a woman right in front of her son wasn't my finest move.

I cleared my throat and willed my body to forget that plan. At least for now. I could hear Bo clomping through the downstairs before he found the box of contractor bags.

"I think painting the vanity is ideal. Perhaps a deep gray?" I stared at the sink, determined not to look at her. I was afraid I'd pull her right back into my arms, her son be damned.

"Yes, sure. Gray." Then Max ducked behind me and out the door.

I squeezed my eyes shut and chastised myself. She was here to work for me, not to get mauled in the bathroom. A commotion out front had me leaving the bathroom finally and finding Max arguing with her son. In the front parking lot sat a beat-up silver sedan with country music blaring out the open windows. Colby and Gator peered through the windshield, their heads turning as if watching a tennis match.

"I thought you needed help!"

Max put her hands on her hips. "Yes, *your* help, son."

"I figured three would be better than one. We could get done faster." Bo had an innocent expression on his face that I probably wore when I was that age too. It spelled trouble.

"And why do you want to be done faster?"

Bo spread his arms wide. "Just want to beat the heat, Mama."

Max shook her head. "You're a terrible liar. You have plans with these two, don't you?"

Bo shrugged. "It is Friday night…"

Max rolled her eyes and then dropped her hands. "Fine. Get

them in here, finish the job, and then get out of here, but if I find out you boys are causing trouble, you're grounded. Do you understand me?"

Bo threw his arms around his mom's neck and kissed the top of her head. "Understood. I won't disappoint you."

"Mhm." Max hugged him back and then pushed him off. "You stink."

"See?" Bo's grin probably landed him all the young ladies in town. "Already working hard."

Max scoffed and then marched back in the house, grabbing the front of my shirt and dragging me to the back stairs. "Take down all the drywall downstairs and haul it out but don't mess up the electrical!" she called over her shoulder to the boys.

"You sure this is a good idea?" I asked quietly, following her up the stairs and wondering if she'd just invited trouble into my new business venture. Max seemed to have a good relationship with her son, though I wasn't so sure about the other two boys. Still, she knew them better than me, so if she was okay with things, I'd keep my nose out of it.

"Yeah, they'll be fine. I'm more worried about what they'll do once they leave here." Max spun in a circle in the cleaned out apartment. She seemed to have forgotten about the incident in the bathroom. Maybe that was a good thing. "This space looks great!"

I nodded, seeing that Bo had indeed done a good job. "Roofers come tomorrow. But now we need help in here. Unless you know how to hang drywall?"

Max lifted her arm and crooked her elbow, flexing her bicep. There was a teeny tiny bump there that only made her more attractive. "Heck, yes I can hang drywall."

I grinned back. "Okay, muscles."

"It is officially quitting time," I announced, pulling the broom from Max's hands. "Both upstairs and down are completely cleared, thanks to you and Bo."

Max looked pleased, but exhausted. "Don't forget your own contribution, Prince Cav."

My spine straightened, the hair on the back of my neck rising in distrust. "Why did you just call me that?"

Max laughed, heading over to the wash station, looking unperturbed. "Seems like you come from a well off family, and don't forget all the madam stuff and your accent." She shrugged, drying her hands. "Just seems like 'prince' fits you."

I washed my hands and tried to tell myself to settle down. Max didn't know anything about my real family because I hadn't shared anything. Waiting for my parents to send another person here to drag me back home made me anxious.

A car pulling up outside had me lifting my head. "That must be dinner."

"Dinner?" Max looked confused.

"You said you didn't have a shift at the diner tonight and I know Bo is out with his friends, so I figured I'd get us dinner. Unless you'd rather be home." I didn't want her to feel obligated to be here.

Max smiled shyly at me. "No, no. I'd love to stay."

"Bo educated me on this app on my phone that could have food delivered." Americans and their conveniences never failed to interest me.

Max studied me like she thought I was crazy, but also kind of wonderful. If I could manage normal dinner conversation tonight maybe I could convince her to think of me as more of the latter instead of the former.

I grabbed the two bags that were delivered from a local fish house from the front doorstep and escorted my lovely dinner companion to my truck bed. "With the canopy, we can eat without the biting bugs."

"Mosquitoes."

"Yes, that's what I said."

Max burst out laughing but she took my hand to climb up into the truck. With just my sleeping bag, two duffle bags, and a canopy net surrounding us, it wasn't the nicest table I'd ever sat at for dinner, but the view of Max in her turquoise tank top was delightful. We talked the whole time we ate, mostly about construction and plans for this land, but she also told me about her best friend, the other server that night at the diner.

When we both had to lie down due to being so full on shrimp tacos and tortilla chips, Max let me stretch my arm out, giving her my bicep as a pillow. She kept a good two inches between our bodies as we lay there, watching the sky turn dark.

I knew I probably shouldn't ask, but I couldn't keep the question behind my lips any longer. "Is Bo's father around?"

So far I was only familiar with tearing walls down, but I watched in fascination as Max instantly erected walls around herself. Walls to keep me out of this conversation.

"Nope. It's me and Bo, just the way I like it."

"Ah. I see."

"Is Fiona still in town?"

And now I was uncomfortable. "Yes, she's staying at a hotel

for now. She understands I'm not leaving, and she'd like to stay too." I felt Max stiffen and I rushed to add, "Not for me, but to start her own life here. She and I are back to being friends. Only friends."

"Ah."

"Yes, ah." I stared up to the sky as the stars began to appear, one by one. The cicadas started up, as if the first one to start his mating call made all the others do the same. I felt like I needed my own mating call. Clearly, what had worked for me in Mardelvia was not working here in America. I'd never had to look for a date. Available women, while not exactly lined up, had always been easy to come by. Having 'prince' before your name made that a guarantee. Now that I no longer had that title, I wasn't sure what about me was attractive to a woman.

"I feel like I should have more figured out at this point in my life," I said quietly, more to myself than anything.

Max rolled toward me, her body so close now that her knee brushed against the outside of my thigh. "Tell me about it. I still can't believe they let me go home with a baby from the hospital without proper directions. Now that he's a teenager, I really need to have more figured out, but I guess that's the way of it, right?"

"What do you mean?"

Max's head had somehow nestled itself onto my shoulder, her face just inches away from mine. Her eyes sparkled in the moonlight, those lashes sweeping up and down as she talked. I tried to focus on her words and somehow only managed to focus on her lips. The way she bit her puffy bottom one when she was focused on a task. The dip in the top lip, right in the

THE SPARE AND THE SINGLE MOM

center. The way her lips tilted up so prettily when she smiled, which was often.

"No one gives us instructions. That's why our parents messed us up, and why we mess up our own kids. Everyone's just bumbling around, trying to figure things out. By the time we get it all sorted, we die."

"That sounds terrible." My hand came up to push a wayward hair away from her eyes.

"I don't know. They say to love the journey, not the destination, so I guess we have to eke out some kind of enjoyment along the way, right?"

I couldn't agree more. That was the whole point of this trip to America. The whole reason I found myself touching her. I knew I'd find enjoyment.

"Max?" Was it just my imagination or had she rolled closer? I could swear I felt all her curves pressing against my side.

"Yeah?"

"If you don't want to be kissed under the stars right now, you better sit up."

"Oh!" Her eyelids dropped and then they swooped upward again, gaze locking with mine. "I like it right here just fine."

I didn't give her a chance to rethink her answer, I just closed the gap between us, finally pressing my lips to hers and getting my first taste of true freedom. She smelled of flowers and tasted like sweet tea. Her hand gripped my shirt like she was afraid I'd end the kiss too soon. The heat bloomed instantly and after a whimper from the back of her throat, I found myself deepening the kiss. Her lips parted and I dove in deeper, rolling until I was on top of her. Max parted her legs just enough for me to settle between them, wrenching a groan from my mouth. She was perfect. She was everything every woman I'd ever dated was not.

And as the kiss went on, our hands traveling over clothing, exploring and touching, I realized that no matter what happened with this business adventure, as long as Max was here in Sailfish Banks, I would be too.

Chapter Eleven
MAXINE

After I headed home that night, I lay on the couch thinking.

I had a lot on my mind, not the least of which was a certain handsome man who'd kissed me like his life depended on it in the back of a truck under the stars. Cav's kiss had been tentative at first, almost proper–like everything else about him. But when I responded, pressing every inch of myself as close as I could get without actually climbing inside his clothes with him, I'd felt something else. I mean, I'd definitely felt that... but it had also seemed like there was more to this well-mannered and perfectly tailored guy than met the eye. And whatever else there was, it had threatened to come out during that kiss. It was something ferocious and demanding, something very different from the calm and careful man Cav seemed on the outside.

It was fascinating, and as his arms had held me close, his hands tracing every inch of my body while my own hands did a little exploring of their own, I wanted more.

We had made out like teenagers for what felt like hours. I'd eventually rolled Cav to his back and straddled him, pressing myself against him shamelessly, seeking a kind of release I hadn't felt with a man in years. Lord only knew how far we might have gone if Teddy Heffner hadn't chosen that moment to blast down the road in his souped-up Charger, blaring Bon Jovi while his muffler did the opposite of muffling. The sound started us apart, and I'd rolled off Cav, trying to decide if I regretted anything that had happened between us.

I found that I didn't.

I actually found that if Teddy hadn't startled us apart, I would have probably been happy to not regret a whole lot more.

But it was good that we'd stopped. I wasn't some carefree teenager, free to make out in truck beds with handsome men. That was what had gotten me here in the first place. Kind of.

The thing was, it had been different with Bo's daddy. He'd been my age, but he had seemed so much older, more experienced. We'd dated my whole junior year, and I'd been naive enough to have all the usual fantasies. I cringed thinking of it now, the way I'd pasted images of white dresses and flowers into the pages of a notebook, writing my name with his over and over.

It was a first love.

And it was the worst love, too.

Because in the end, it wasn't love at all. At least not for Brody Hawkins.

When I got pregnant, I was sure he'd know what to do. But Brody was a senior, weeks away from graduation. His solution to my "problem" was to take off as soon as school ended. He never told his folks, he never even told me goodbye.

And my own parents?

I could still remember Daddy's face when he told me not to come back. He'd stood in the doorway, his face reddened with anger and sweat beaded on his brow. Mama had hovered just behind him, her hands pressed to her mouth and her eyes red and watery. I'd left that little town that day, taking the few things I actually owned with me to head several towns away to coastal North Carolina to visit the only family I had outside my parents. My great aunt had always been kind to me as a kid. I recall praying the whole bus ride up that she'd still be kind now that I was a pregnant teenager whose parents couldn't see their way to love her anymore.

I sat up, looking around the little cottage that had been my refuge, and my home since I'd arrived in Sailfish Banks. Aunt Glenda was gone, but I still felt her here. Her warm embrace when I'd wandered to her doorstep, terror in my heart and not a dollar to my name. I saw her in the pink paint outside every time I came home. I heard her in the way Bo called me "Mama" when he was sad or sick–she'd taught him to respect his elders, helped me raise him until she'd died. She'd been family to me when my own had abandoned me.

What time was it, anyway? I rose and stretched, checking my watch. After midnight. Bo was nearly eighteen, but we had a deal. He knew I'd wait up, and he knew I didn't do well after midnight. But he still wasn't home.

I shuffled to the kitchen to make a cup of herbal tea. I wouldn't sleep right then anyway. My mind was too busy. It had been strange seeing Cav with Bo. The two of them had been side by side at one point, hunched over as they knelt on the floor, prying up linoleum together. I couldn't hear what they said, but there was a moment where they both burst out laughing, grinning at each other, and my heart had nearly exploded inside my chest. Bo had never had a proper father figure. It was one place I'd failed him, and I'd been trying to make up for that in every other way I could.

But as I'd watched those big strong men side by side, young and eager, mature and seasoned, I realized how much I'd failed to give my son.

"Mama." Bo tiptoed through the front door, coming to a dead stop when he saw me standing at the counter dipping my tea bag. "You're up."

"When have you ever come home to find me not up?"

"It's late."

"No. You're late."

He closed the door softly, turning the deadbolt and shooting me a doleful look. "I lost track of time. I'm sorry."

I regarded him, my eyes roaming the long athletic build, his tattered jeans hugging strong legs and the faded Sailfish Banks T-shirt pulled tight across a chest that was no longer a little boy's. When had he grown up? I'd been watching the whole time, and it still surprised me daily.

"What were you boys up to out there?"

"Bonfire," he told me, his eyes meeting mine and then dancing away. He moved into the kitchen, pulling open the fridge and taking out the milk before pouring himself a glass.

"And?" I asked. I knew very well what happened at the

bonfires down on the north end of the island at Amherst Beach.

Bo sighed. "Three beer maximum. Kept it in my pants. Said please and thank you even though no one else ever does. Made sure I had consent before I touched anyone." He recited the rules back to me in a voice that told me he was annoyed, but that he also believed in these rules enough to follow them.

"Good boy."

Bo put down his milk and turned to face me, his big hands landing on my shoulders. "Mama. I know you worry. But I'm not planning to get into any trouble. I want to make you proud. And someday, I want to set us both up right. I'll take care of you, just like you've always taken care of me."

"You and me," I murmured, repeating the mantra I'd made our reprieve since he was an infant in my arms. "Just you and me."

He hugged me tight and I felt him nod above my head. "Though maybe it could be you and me and... Cav?"

I froze and pulled out of his embrace. "What?"

"I see how you guys are," he said, clearly aware this was new territory for us. "I just thought maybe–"

"Well, quit thinking." I snapped.

"Mama," my son said softly, picking up his glass. "I hate the idea of you being alone forever."

"We need to get to bed. Roofers come tomorrow." I turned away from Bo, leaving the remnants of my tea on the counter. My mind was already in a twist, and Bo's words only made it worse.

The thing was, I didn't want to be alone forever either. But I wasn't sure I was brave enough for anything else.

"I had no idea it would be so noisy," Cav shouted. We faced each other inside the open space of the building we'd cleared. The roof was being replaced above us, and with no carpet or furnishings to absorb the noise, it was like being inside an echo chamber. The plan had been to hang drywall inside while they worked out there, but my head was pounding and it seemed Cav had the same problem.

"It is pretty awful," I said. "I didn't bring the muffs today either." I wore them with power tools, and my ears wished I'd planned better.

"We should get out of here," Cav said, taking my hand and pulling me out the front door and down the steps.

I followed willingly, trying not to think about how it felt to have my hand in his, trying not to consider other places I'd like that hand to touch, and doing my best not to think about the kiss under the stars the night before.

It wasn't that I didn't like Cav. That was definitely not the problem. It was more that I didn't trust him completely. He'd come out of nowhere, and I had no reason to believe he wouldn't head right on back there just as easy as he'd come.

Sure I liked the guy. And he was great with my son. But I didn't want either of us to get attached. History didn't lie, and there was no denying that men and Max were not a good combination.

Just as Cav and I reached the curb, Fiona appeared, strolling up the sidewalk on the other side of the street, a parasol open over her perfectly coiffed light hair, and her body looking all long and lean in a fitted sheath dress. She definitely didn't fit in here in Sailfish Banks, and from the way Angus was ogling her from where he sat on his front porch, I wasn't the only one who noticed.

"Hello, Pr-er..." she stopped, looking both ways and crossing the street to meet us. "Cav. Max."

"Hey Fi," I said, pulling my hand from Cav's. I still wasn't sure what exactly went on between these two before they showed up here, but I was certain they were made for one another. Prim, proper, scented lightly of money... why in the world had Cav been kissing me?

"Your little project is creating quite a ruckus," she said. "I could hear it from three blocks away."

"Far worse inside, I'm afraid," Cav said. "I fear we won't be accomplishing much today."

He wasn't wrong, and maybe it was for the best. I imagined Cyrus would get back to me with a crew Monday or Tuesday anyway–he always said a month but it never took that long–and I'd make more on the referral fees than I would if I hung drywall myself. The smart thing would've been for me to excuse myself and head home. I had the day off again, something that worried me a little bit. I rarely had two weekend days off, and it made me think maybe the owner of the diner had gotten tired of me. Had he found someone else?

I shoved that thought aside. Franny would certainly tell me. She worked every day, just like me most of the time, and she was my best friend. I'd know if there was trouble, I figured. So I decided to just enjoy the free time. And if we weren't going to be hanging drywall...

"You two ever been to a carnival?" I asked Cav and Fiona.

They exchanged a look that told me they definitely had not. "You know, fried Snickers bars, ring tossing games, rides?"

"I'm certain we haven't," Cav said.

I grinned at him. "No reason to be afraid, Prince Cav." Cav did that weird stiffening thing again at the nickname I'd given him, and even Fiona seemed taken aback by it.

"Did you–?"

"Yep, I dubbed him Prince Cav. He's got a princely way about him, don't you think? Very regal." I looked to Fiona for agreement.

"He does, you're right," she said, a little smile playing on her pretty lips. "And I am very curious about this fried bar you mentioned. I've heard that Americans can fry anything to eat."

"Very true." I gestured toward my SUV. "It's just one county over. If you're up for it, let's go."

They exchanged another glance I couldn't decipher, and we piled into my car, heading for the Conklin County Carnival. It was either the best or the worst idea I'd ever had, but I couldn't help wanting to spend more time with Cav. And with Fiona too. They were part of a world I knew nothing about, and even though my experience was limited, my curiosity was huge.

We pulled into the crowded parking lot forty-five minutes later, and my passengers both gaped from their open windows.

"It looks like the London Eye, only tiny," Fiona said, pointing out the window.

"That," I told her, "is the Conklin County Carnival Ferris wheel. And it will definitely be on the agenda today."

As we locked the car and turned to head to the entrance gate, Fiona walked just ahead of us and Cav took my hand again. My heart flip-flopped inside me, and I took a deep breath. I didn't know what I was doing, but it might already have been too late to stop. I swallowed hard and told myself to hold on tight. This was one ride I hadn't been on before.

Chapter Twelve
CAVANAUGH

Poor Fiona. Her silk dress was sticking to her skin. She kept pulling it away from her body and fanning herself. She was still dressing like a debutante looking to catch the eye of a prince while melting in the hot North Carolina sun. "You didn't go to Wallie?"

Fiona winced, creeping ahead in line. "The fabrics were interesting."

Max put her hand on me, leaning around my side to speak to Fiona. "You might like the mall better. They have some department stores that carry nice clothes, but perhaps more suitable for the summers here."

Fiona smiled gratefully. "Thank you. I'll give that a try." Her gaze dropped to our hands, where our fingers had been laced together all afternoon. "So is this official? You two?"

"Yes."

"Well..."

Max and I spoke at the same time. I glanced down at her. "This is most definitely official. Do Americans need some sort of ring? Or a promise? Or a public declaration to make it official?"

Max's cheeks had gone pink but that could have been from the heat. "I mean, not really. But maybe a conversation about it would be appropriate?"

I nodded. "I vote yes for making it official."

Max sputtered, flicking a glance at Fiona. "Perhaps we should talk about this later?"

"You mean because of me?" Fiona grabbed Max's arm. "I think you two are wonderful together. I've never seen Cavanaugh so relaxed and happy. In fact, I'm not sure he smiled at all the last few years."

I frowned, wondering if that was true. I'd been unhappy, but I thought I'd hid it well.

"Are you sure? It sounded like you two were engaged." Max trailed off.

"Oh, goodness, no. Never engaged. More like our families promised us each other, but then we realized we don't want each other?" Fiona's eyes went wide. "Not that I don't like you, Cavanaugh, but we're so much better as friends."

"See?" I said to Max. "Friends. Just like I told you. So no reason you and I cannot be official."

"Great! Then it's settled." Fiona beamed while Max opened and closed her mouth several times.

"Next!"

Fiona gasped and turned, stepping into the waiting basket of the Ferris wheel. "See you at the top!" And then her basket whisked away, another one arriving in its place and a couple getting out.

I held my hand out and let Max climb in first. I followed,

finding very little room to move once the bar over our laps came down and the contraption shifted us into the air. I put my hand on the sticky bar and looked over the edge at the steady stream of people walking on the hot blacktop, stopping to buy food from the vendors or waiting in line for rides. A child in a stroller screamed at his parents, probably wanting to go home to air conditioning. Another child burst into tears as her ice cream scoop fell off her cone and began to melt on the ground.

"This is what people do in America during the summer?"

Max chuckled. "Just wait until we're at the top. You'll see."

It took quite a long time to get to the top, but when we did, I welcomed the cool breeze on my face. Not a single sound from below traveled up to us. It was like we were on our own little metal island up here at the top of the Ferris wheel. I could see the ocean to my right, the white caps gently rocking toward shore.

"What is the American thing to do at the top of the Ferris wheel? Say cheers? High five?" Bo had shown me some sort of knuckle banging thing yesterday, but I wasn't sure that was appropriate with a lady I was trying to woo.

Max ducked her head, a smile spread across her pretty face. "Kiss."

I leaned closer, ignoring the view outside our bucket. "Did you say kiss?"

She nodded, looking up at me through her lashes. She did not have to say it twice. I leaned down and pushed her hair away from her neck, cupping her jaw and tilting her head to the side. My lips landed on hers none too gently due to the Ferris wheel jerking us downward. The world swooped away and it may have been the kiss or it could have been the ride. Either way, I was lost in this woman. Her hands slid up my arms and around my neck, holding me closer. The cool breeze couldn't cool off the heat between us as her tongue dueled with mine. Max was no innocent debutante, too shy to take what she wanted. And somehow, some way, Max wanted me.

"Uh, guys?"

A voice interrupted our kiss. We both twisted our heads to see the young man who'd helped us get into the Ferris wheel. He'd averted his gaze, but his thumb was tapping impatiently against his thigh.

"Ride's over, folks."

I cleared my throat and pulled away from Max as she scrambled to tug on the bottom of her shirt and smooth out her hair. The lap bar lifted easily and I helped her climb out. The kid shot me a wink behind Max's back, which made me shake my head. I hadn't meant to let things go that far on the ride, but every time I got my hands on Max, I lost my head.

"Wasn't that amazing?" Fiona exclaimed, having waited for us at the exit of the ride.

"It really was," Max replied, hugging my arm and staring up at me. I was pretty sure she didn't mean the ride.

"If you don't mind, I'm going to get a ride back to the hotel. I would like to get to the mall tomorrow for better clothing and then I need to buy all the things you'll need for the new bar, Cavanaugh. Your parents have not shut down my credit card yet."

I winced. I'd completely forgotten about my parents in the thrill of building my new business and whatever this was with Max. Speaking of, Max was looking at me funny. Perhaps freely handing out credit cards was not done here in America. "Mother's patience will not last much longer."

Fiona's hands twisted together. "Then we better get that bar built fast."

She took off, promising to text us when she got back to the hotel safely. Max and I walked around the carnival hand in hand, stopping to play some of the games. When I won a huge stuffed bear for shooting out the tin cans a mere ten feet from me, Max seemed delighted. She would be ecstatic to see the deer heads on the wall at the hunting lodge back home that I'd been responsible for taking down on horseback. Somehow the cheap teddy bear seemed like a better prize.

We'd shared a fried Twinkie and I was sporting the stomachache to prove it when the storm clouds pushed in. A crack of lightning was the only warning we got before the clouds opened up and dumped on us. Max squealed and we began to run for the exit along with all the other carnival goers. Before we made it to her car, we were soaked to the skin. I found myself laughing as we ran, slipping and sliding in the parking lot that had turned to mud. At the car, I threw her bear in the back and pressed Max up against her door. I kissed her like my life depended on it. She melted against me, both of us oblivious to the warm rain pelting our skin.

"What was that for?" she asked, voice raised over the sound of rain hitting the roof of the SUV.

I shrugged, grinning down at her. "I'm happy, I guess."

Max answered my grin with one of hers. "Happy looks good on you, Prince Cav."

Max drove us home, our clothes drying out with the windows rolled down once the rain had stopped. I didn't know how a place could be so wet and yet be so hot. I associated rain with cold, winter weather, but North Carolina was very different. As we pulled into the parking lot of my building, I did a double take. There were white streamers all across the front of the building, the edges of my brand new roof, and even the huge oak tree out front.

"What is this?"

Max burst out laughing, putting the car in park. "Oh, he'll wish he never messed with us."

I climbed out of the car, thoroughly confused. "Who? And what is this decoration?"

Max only laughed harder. "You just got TP'd, Cav. I'd bet money it was Angus."

I turned to her, still confused. "Angus? The toilet scavenger?"

"Yeah, well, you gave him a toilet. He gave you toilet paper."

I touched the streamer across the front door. It was indeed toilet paper. How very odd Americans were. "Do we keep it?"

Max let out a snort from laughing so hard. "No! We'll take it down tomorrow when it's dry. Believe me, you don't want to try to take down wet toilet paper."

I spun toward her. "You've had this done to you before?"

"Oh, Cav. You have so much to learn about friendly neighbor rivalry."

I shook my head slowly, staring at toilet paper strewn about my new home. "I guess I do."

Max hooked her thumb over her shoulder. "I better get home before Bo starts calling around, looking for me."

"I will take you." I dug in my pockets for the keys to my truck.

"No, it's okay. I have my car."

I abandoned the key search to cup Max's face in my hands. "I do not understand toileting someone's house, but I do know how to treat a lady. I will follow you home so I know you got back safely."

Her shoulders seemed to unglue from her ears. I had a feeling Max usually carried the weight of the world on her shoulders. If this one small thing would help, I would do it. "Okay."

"Okay." I kissed the tip of her nose, not trusting myself to kiss her lips.

I followed her home, waiting until she waved from the front doorstep and went inside before sputtering away from the curb and heading home again. Despite the rain and the surprise toilet paper, I'd had the best day of my life.

"Hey, Cavvy!"

I put down the huge piece of drywall I'd carried from the back of my truck. I hadn't been able to sleep well so the minute the hardware store was open, I'd been there to buy a whole truck bed worth of drywall. Fiona was right. I needed to get this place in working order sooner rather than later, and on a personal level, I wanted to buy some furniture for the upstairs apartment. I couldn't very well keep making out with Max in the back of my truck like some bedless teenager.

"Hello, Ben." I dusted off my hands and shook his when he stretched it out. "We're making quite a bit of headway with this building."

Ben pulled a baseball cap out of his truck and put it on his head. He stretched his beefy arms out wide. "And now that I'm here with the tractor, we'll make some headway on the rental units, baby."

I glanced over at the trailer he was pulling behind his truck. The tractor looked like it could chew up this land in a matter of minutes. "You know how to run that thing?"

Ben smirked. "Come on, Cav. I've been helping Dad since I was a boy. His company might be big enough that he and I don't have to get our hands dirty, but I still know how to run a tractor with my eyes closed."

"Do not run the tractor with your eyes closed, I beg of you."

Ben slapped me on the shoulder. "You always were funny, Cav. I'm real glad you're here. Chance to get to know each other and all that. Plus, I think I have a proposition for these rentals that might intrigue you. Dad ever hand over the deed?"

I frowned, having forgotten about that too. So many details to starting and running your own company. "No, not yet. I will call him today."

Ben nodded. "Just don't have him come out here until I'm gone. He still thinks I'm pushing paper at the home office."

I nodded and let Ben get to work. The tractor was revving and beeping all day long while I attacked the upstairs apartment. Max came over for a few hours, proving that she lived up to her nickname by holding drywall while I screwed it in. Of course, I kept missing the studs or mangling the drywall, so Max had to take over the screwdriver while I held the drywall.

"Might have to put a bathtub in here so you can soak those

tired arms, muscles," I whispered in her ear before kissing her neck.

Max giggled softly. "Maybe you'll have to massage them instead."

I leaned the next piece of drywall against the wall and pressed Max into the wall we'd just hung. "I don't know, gorgeous. I prefer naked massages. You up for that?"

She walked her fingers up my shoulders and into my hair. "I could be convinced..."

My hand slid under her shirt and up her torso. She bit her bottom lip, our eyes locked on each other. An inch north and her breast rested in my palm, a heat rock of luscious curves that had me hard in a split second. Max's tongue darted out to lick her lips and I decided we should christen the room right bloody now, even if only half the drywall was in.

"Got the damn wheel stuck. Can you–" Ben's voice trailed off.

I whipped my hand out of Max's shirt but not before Ben saw exactly what we were up to.

"Uh, sorry. I can, uh, go." He averted his eyes, scratching at the five o'clock shadow that had crossed the line into beard territory.

Max tugged at her shirt and slipped around me. "No, it's okay. I have to get to my shift at the diner anyway. See you tomorrow, Cav?"

I had to adjust my jeans before I could speak. "Might come in for dinner later, if that's alright."

Max smiled so prettily at that suggestion I knew I'd make it there for dinner even if I had to drink a gallon of coffee to keep my eyes open. She left and Ben looked at me apologetically.

"Sorry, man. Had no idea that was going on. You two an item?"

"Most definitely."

Ben nodded. "Nice work, Cav. Max is great."

I didn't want him talking about how great Max was or how pretty or how knowledgeable. I wanted to keep her all to myself for now. "Did you need some help with the tractor?"

We both worked outside the rest of the day, sweat dripping down our backs as we cleared half of the extra land. When the sun started to dip in the sky, Ben shut down the tractor and said he'd be back the day after tomorrow to finish the rest. I headed inside to try to bathe in the tiny wash station Max had set up. After a change of clothes, I went into the bathroom to comb my hair so I didn't look homeless when I went to see her at the diner.

My gaze snagged on a bright pink sticky note on the mirror with Max's handwriting on it.

My heart is open and I am attracting trusting relationships.

I let that one sink in, knowing this was a glimpse into how she was feeling, while also being a warning. Max was letting me in and I'd better be trustworthy. I wasn't quite there yet as far as being one hundred percent honest about my family, but I felt the same way. My heart was open and I knew it was falling for Max.

Chapter Thirteen
MAXINE

"Order's up, Max!"

I hustled around the counter to pick up the grilled cheese and burgers the cook had slid under the heat lamps and delivered them to the group of local guys waiting in the corner booth.

"You got some kinda new job going on, Max?" one of the guys asked as I placed a burger before him. I knew him, but I couldn't remember his name.

I put a hand on my hip and inspected the group. Two of the guys had been in school with me that horrible senior year when my belly had been ballooning out at an alarming rate and my teen pregnancy had been the subject of at least eighty percent of the local gossip. Aunt Glenda had insisted I finish high school, though I had not been excited about her plan. Now though? I was glad I'd done it.

These guys were trades, I knew. Electricians, plumbers, all around construction guys who I'd worked with before.

"Yep. Pretty big project over at the old Daniels Donuts. Cyrus talk to you?" I asked.

The guy who'd asked the question couldn't answer, since he had a burger dangling from his face, but one of the other guys, Ritchie, did. "Headed over there this afternoon," he said. "Sounds like there's a lot going on."

I relaxed a bit. I was still never sure around town if I was about to be the butt of some joke, and when I didn't feel like I was the one in charge of the conversation, my insecurities made me defensive. But these guys weren't here to give me a hard time. They were working for Cyrus, which meant they were working for Cav. And for me.

I filled them in on the specifics of the job, enjoying talking–even in this somewhat unrelated way–about Cav, who I found myself thinking about constantly.

"Look lively, darlin'," Franny said, passing by. "New table by the door."

I shot my best friend a smile, and left the guys to help the new customers who'd just come in. The lunch hour was packed, and a few hours slid by easily, filled with drinks and slices of pie. By the time I had a moment to think again, Franny and I were both leaning against the diner's long counter, side by side, sipping sweet teas.

"You getting all the hours you usually do?" I asked her, trying not to let worry seep into my voice.

"Yeah, why?"

"Just wasn't sure why I was off the schedule all weekend," I said.

Franny scanned my face, and I could see her thinking. "I

figured you asked for it. Maybe something to do with the handsome man staying out at the Daniels place?"

I hadn't mentioned Cav to my best friend, and turned fully to face her now. Had there been gossip? "How do you know about him?"

She sputtered out a laugh, reaching one hand out to squeeze my shoulder. "Honey, you should see your face."

"I don't like people discussing my business."

"Don't I know it!" She shook her head and sipped her tea before putting it down and turning to face me. "There's little chance of a fancy package of a man like that coming to town without there being plenty of talk. You oughta know that."

That made sense. Of course Cav would inspire curiosity around a small town like this.

"But the way you just stiffened up... Honey, is there something going on with you?"

I didn't answer right away, and my hesitation spoke more than words could have.

"Ooh, Max, you've been holding out on me!" Franny bounced on her toes, her eyes bright with excitement. "Come on, spill. I have to live vicariously. You know there's nothing going on with me and Hot Al back at home."

Franny and Alfonse had been the "it" couple that final year in high school. Homecoming king and queen, football captain and pep squad princess. But they were local, and they stayed local, neither dreaming of any kind of life outside of Sailfish Banks. And they seemed happy here, even if "Hot Al" seemed a little less hot in his midlife years than he had as a hunky high school senior. Franny had been kind to me back then, and she was still my best friend today.

"I'm not sure what's going on exactly," I told her.

"I know it's been a while. Do you need me to walk you through the mechanics of it all?" She smiled deviously and I whacked her with my order pad.

"Definitely not." I sighed, deciding how much to tell her. Part of me was desperate to talk about Cav, but part of me wanted to keep it all to myself. "His name is Cavanaugh Barclay. He's Leo Barclay's nephew, and he's from some far away country he refers to as a 'kingdom.'"

"What?" Franny squawked. "That's amazing. Maybe he's like a duke or something!"

I tilted my head. He might be, I thought. "I call him Prince Cav because he's very proper and pulled together. All the manners, you know."

She nodded eagerly. "Cloth napkins and handkerchiefs, I bet."

"Yes, definitely." I took a deep breath. "Anyway, he's renovating the old Daniels Donuts to be a bar and a little park of rental properties, and I'm helping him. And we've... kind of... gotten close." I thought about the easy and sudden way Cav had claimed me in front of Fiona. It had been a little abrupt, I thought, but once he'd announced that we were a couple, I didn't feel any need to argue. "Anway, we're kind of... dating, I guess."

"Oh, if you could see the pink in your cheeks right now," Franny said, clearly enjoying this. "So is it serious?"

I shook my head. "Of course not, no. He just got here. I barely know the guy."

"Have you, ah...?"

I'd definitely thought about sex with Cav. But sex was not

something I took lightly. I knew the potential consequences of being spontaneous better than anyone. And more importantly, I knew what it was to give your heart to someone who didn't value it or who had other plans that didn't include you. "Not yet."

She grinned, her eyes darting over my shoulder and then returning to my face. "Does he like your burgers or your grilled cheese better?" There was a teasing note in her voice I didn't quite understand.

"What?"

"Well, whatever you've been giving him, he's back for more, darlin'." She squeezed my hand and angled her head to the door. I spun around to find Cav standing just inside the door, Ben at his side.

Despite my hesitation about whatever this thing was between us, my heart inflated inside my chest, and I imagined that my face showed every bit of the adoration I'd begun to feel for my very own Prince Cav. And every single time I saw him, it was like the first time all over again. I was struck by his mass of sexy dark hair, that one lock falling over his forehead. Those soulful dark eyes, and the build that towered over me and reminded me that no matter how proper he might seem, he was one hundred percent man. A little shiver ran through me at the thought.

"Hey, y'all," I said, pulling myself together and stepping closer, picking up two menus on my way.

Cav stepped forward, leaning down to give me a sweet kiss on the cheek. "Hi beautiful."

"Max," Ben said. "Hi."

"You looking for an early dinner?" I asked them, waving them into a booth.

"I was looking for you," Cav told me. "But a piece of pie wouldn't be unwelcome."

As they sat, Cav filled me in on the property.

"Ben cleared the whole lot, and Cyrus brought at least ten men over today," Cav said. "They were busy immediately, in the main building and also digging foundations for the outbuildings. Lots of machinery and sweaty men. Lots of noise."

"That's great," I said, glad to hear that Cyrus had organized so much help. "That'll get things moving."

Cav was looking at me with a strange expression, and when I delivered their pie, he rose. "Might we have a quick word?" He glanced around and I followed his gaze to see Franny grinning at us from the counter. She shot us a thumbs-up that I could feel turning my cheeks bright red.

"Yeah, of course." I led Cav to the back of the restaurant. Technically, guests were not supposed to be in the back, but I wasn't worried.

The second we were alone, he pulled me into his arms, those fierce lips of his finding mine and sending full-body shivers racing through me. He kissed me like a man seeking life, like a man about to be sent to the gallows or on a long voyage. And I kissed him back the same way, wishing I could wrap myself around him. Even though my brain was screaming at me to be cautious, there were other parts of me that suggested caution was for prudes. And those parts thrilled when his hands pulled my skirt up my thighs and slid up the back of my legs to cup my ass.

Finally, he broke away, leaving me breathless.

"I missed you," he said, his dark eyes gleaming.

"I missed you too," I admitted.

"And I wanted to see if you'd be willing to go furniture shopping with me tonight."

"Tonight?"

He nodded. "Ben says the furniture store down the island takes at least a week to get things delivered. And the guys working on the apartment said they'd have floors in by then. So I'd like to get a bed and a dresser at least. Maybe some kitchen things."

"Tired of the truck?"

He pressed his forehead to mine. "I like it better when you're in it with me." He stared into my eyes for a long moment. "And I suspect I'll like it much better when we're in a proper bed."

A thrill chased concern through my chest. I wanted to have sex with Cav. The minor explosions happening inside my body were proof of that. But I was also scared. I'd had sex since Bo's dad, of course. But not with anyone I cared about at all. And that was by design. But sex with Cav? I worried it would mean something. And that would just give him the power to hurt me.

"So?" he asked, pulling me from my worries.

"I mean... yes," I said slowly, realizing I was just putting myself into a position to be hurt. But I couldn't help it. I wanted to be closer to this man. "I'd like that. I've been thinking about it too," I confessed.

A little smile lifted one side of his sculpted lips. "You're not talking about furniture shopping right now, are you?"

Oh crap. I dropped my head. "Um. No. The other thing."

"You have no idea how excited I am to hear you say that," he said, pulling me close again.

"I have some idea," I told him, wiggling my hips against the iron rod pressed against me.

He kissed me once more, carefully and sweetly this time. And then he let me go, tugging at his jeans and smoothing his T-shirt over his muscled chest. "Furniture first. Then we'll get to that," he said, his cultured accent nearly taking my knees out from beneath me.

I felt the hesitation building in my chest, and Cav waited patiently, seeming to sense that I had something to say. "It just..." I began. "It's been a long time. And it's hard for me to..."

"I don't think you'll have any problems with that," Cav assured me, looking smug.

"Not that," I snapped. "It's hard for me to trust. Men. Specifically."

"Oh." His grip around me tightened, but his face softened. "That makes sense," he said. "I don't know all the details, of course... but if Bo's father..."

"Exactly. And my own daddy too. Men don't tend to stick long where I'm concerned."

"Well, I'm not going anywhere." The words were right, but I worried that he could disappear just as suddenly as he'd appeared here. "So. Furniture?"

"Sounds good," I said, working to push the worry from my mind. He was here. He was handsome. And for whatever reason, he was interested in me.

"I've also been doing some research," he told me.

"Oh really?" I asked, as we moved back out into the restaurant.

"Yes, and I'm going to buy some eggs."

"Omelet research?"

"Egging research. We're going to extract our revenge on Angus."

I frowned. "Eggs are really hard to clean up. He might just escalate things from there."

"You have a better idea?" he asked.

"I'll think on it," I told him. "You don't want to strike back right away. He'll be expecting that. The trick is to catch him unawares."

"Unawares," Cav said, nodding.

"Why do I sense that the two of you are up to no good?" Ben asked us.

"You're welcome to join the fun," Cav said.

"Ah, no," Ben said. "Not into the threesome thing, but thanks."

I felt the blood rush to my face, and decided that was a good time to attend to my other customers.

Chapter Fourteen
CAVANAUGH

"Be quiet or you'll get us caught!" I whispered loudly as Max stumbled, looking like she might fall on the ground from laughing so hard.

She'd come over before dawn as I'd requested, looking adorably sleepy. I took the jug from her unstable hands and pushed her over by Angus's fence to help her stay upright. She wasn't going to be much help, but I loved to hear her laugh. I stayed in a crouch the whole time I tipped over the jug and poured the liquid on Angus's grass. It was hard to know if I was getting the shape just right, but I did my best and somehow got us out of there before Angus woke up and noticed giggling trespassers.

Back at my place, I buried the jug in the oversized dumpster I'd rented to hold all the material we'd torn out of the building during demolition. The crew would be showing up soon and I wanted to steal a private moment with Max before they crawled all over the property. I pressed her up against my truck and familiarized myself with her lips again. Each time we'd been alone, we'd gone further and further, both of us pulling away with heaving lungs and a desire for more.

"What did we even do? Water his grass?" Max was still amused, her fingers digging into the back of my hair.

I didn't want to talk about Angus and this ridiculous neighborly prank situation that Max had assured me was just how people did things around here. "Nah, just some weed killer specifically not for grass."

Max gasped. "You're diabolical! You destroyed his whole lawn?"

I shrugged. "Not his whole lawn. Just drew a fun shape out front." I dipped my head and kissed that spot on her neck that always made her body go soft against mine. "Enough about Angus, yes?"

She let out a soft sigh, tipping her head back to give me more room. "Definitely yes."

A loud horn interrupted the best part of my day and had my head lifting. Max's cheeks went pink like they always did when we got caught making out like teens. Ben bounced his truck into the parking lot, smiling and waving out the open window. Despite his poor timing, I'd enjoyed getting to know my cousin better the last few days. He was a jokester, something I was not used to. The royal family was not known for telling jokes or laughing much, sadly. The stress of the job and keeping up appearances had bled the joy out of our family, something I intended to go against with the family I made here in America.

"Hey, love birds." Ben climbed out of the truck and tossed me a grin. "We're pouring concrete today so unless you want to stick around for that mess, you might want to take the day off."

"I have the early lunch shift anyway," Max answered.

"How about I finish painting upstairs so we're ready for the furniture delivery, and we'll meet up again after your shift?"

Max lifted onto her toes to press a quick kiss on my mouth. "Sounds good. I'll bring the cheeseburgers."

I grinned, reluctantly letting her go. I'd come to love greasy cheeseburgers, a delight we did not have in Mardelvia. At least not one the palace chef would make. "I'll miss you."

"And I'll miss you."

"Jesus..." Ben muttered.

I didn't even lift my head to look at him. "Your fault for getting here early."

Max laughed and climbed into her car, tan legs making me wish for more alone time with her. I knew she'd been worried about her lack of shifts lately, but I was hoping the money Cyrus promised he'd pay her would be enough to cover the slow down in tips. I waved as she left, then gave my attention to Ben. He was studying me like I'd grown an extra head overnight.

"Man, I never thought I'd live to see the day."

He was going to give me crap about Max, a move that would make me feel like I needed to defend her. I hoped he didn't go too far because I had zero interest in starting a fist fight with the man. He was bigger and taller than me and probably did more hand-to-hand training while I was stuck fencing. I was coming to find out that many of the skills I'd been taught growing up as a royal were worthless in real life.

"What's on your mind, Benedict?"

He lifted an eyebrow at my use of his full name. "Just didn't think Prince Cavanaugh would be roughing it in the back of a truck in North Carolina while he gets his hands under the skirt of the local waitress."

"Watch what you're saying about her," I warned.

He held his hands up. "I'm not saying anything except that you've changed. The kid I knew who ordered me to tie his shoelace when we were traipsing to the beach all those years ago is gone."

I winced. I didn't recall ordering him to tie my shoe, but that wouldn't have been an odd thing. My parents had enough staff around to make even the most mundane tasks someone else's business to take care of. But Ben was right. I was different. I could feel it already. Just a few weeks here had changed everything.

"I think I love her, Ben."

He clapped me on the back. "I wish you well. I'll just be over here staying single and stealing all the ladies who come sniffing around you."

"No one's sniffing," I scoffed.

Ben chuckled. "Oh, they're sniffing you out alright. Had at least three women corner me just yesterday asking about you. Taking one of them on a date tonight, actually."

I shook my head and laughed. "Thanks for taking one for the team. Hey, speaking of women, did I ever introduce you to Fiona? She needs a place to stay and I wanted to give her one of the first rentals you're working on."

"Nah, don't recall a Fiona, but is she pretty?"

The rest of the crew turned into the parking lot and I tucked that away for later. Fiona and Ben kept missing each other, but I'd need them to meet sooner or later if Fiona was to rent one of the tiny houses Ben was building. Any day now, my parents would cut off her credit cards and she'd have nowhere to stay. Waiting for them to appear and force the confrontation about my disappearance was giving me a daily headache. I wasn't trying to escape them forever, I just needed to have my business up and running by the time we had that confrontation.

I spent the morning rolling paint in the upstairs apartment. I didn't understand why they didn't make paint rollers that would go all the way to the ceiling. I'd have to come back later and try to touch that part up with a brush. At noon I left to meet Uncle Leo at the yacht club for lunch. He'd insisted on taking me to lunch while he handed over the deed for the land. I climbed into my truck and found another sticky note on my steering wheel.

We choose what life we want.

I tucked that one away in my glove box. I was choosing a new life, that was for sure. I just hoped Max would always be a part of it.

When I got to the yacht club, Uncle Leo was waiting outside for me, his polo shirt and black jeans looking sharper than my wrinkled shirt. I'd been to a laundromat in town to get the dirt and stink out of my clothes, but I couldn't do much about the wrinkles. My mother would faint if she saw me looking disheveled. Uncle Leo raised an eyebrow but he didn't faint. We just shook hands and stepped inside the cooled restaurant. The hostess jumped to seat us, clearly knowing Uncle Leo well. I had to stop myself from gulping the ice water. It was a hot day already and I had more work in front of me.

"I appreciate you meeting me, Uncle Leo. We've gotten quite a bit of work done to the property."

He tapped his knuckles against the linen tablecloth without answering. I could tell something was on his mind. All the dread and anxiety I'd been pushing back came flooding in.

"Just got off the phone with your father this morning."

A dozen scenarios raced through my mind, none of them good. "What did you tell him?"

Uncle Leo waited while the server delivered a plate of calamari to our table. I normally loved the stuff, but my stomach was currently tied in knots. When the server left, Uncle Leo huffed.

"He's not happy and he knows you're here. Said they lost all communication with Fiona so they assumed you got to her too."

Bloody hell. I'd have to warn Fiona.

"I told him I was just as surprised as him to know you were here. Also told him he needs to come up with a damn good public reason for your extended leave of absence."

I nodded, swallowing hard. "That's good. Thank you for your discretion."

Uncle Leo threw a piece of calamari in his mouth and chewed before answering. "I won't lie for you, Cav, but I see enough of me in you that I'll keep the royal sharks at bay as long as I can."

"I appreciate that."

Uncle Leo slid an envelope from his back pocket and laid it on the table, his beefy index finger pinning it to the tablecloth. "The property is yours."

"I appreciate–"

He cut me off. "But only if you tell me why my son is always at your property instead of my office."

I ground my molars together. Why was family so damn difficult sometimes? I leaned forward, putting my elbows on the table and squaring off with the man who could ruin all my plans here in America.

"You aren't the only one keeping the sharks at bay, it's just that sometimes they aren't royals."

Uncle Leo narrowed his eyes, looking like he wanted to punch my face in, but I wasn't getting in the middle of whatever was going on with Ben and his father. I had enough of my own family trouble to deal with. Uncle Leo must have come to a conclusion of sorts because he let the envelope go and sat back in his chair.

"You're damn lucky I like you, Cav."

I sat back too, taking the envelope and tucking it into my pocket for safekeeping, hoping he didn't see the way my hand shook. "I'm the lucky one to have you."

Uncle Leo harrumphed but we put that unpleasantness behind us and talked about the property and what I had planned for it. He gave me some great advice and asked to come check it out in a few days. We shook hands after we finished lunch and I breathed a sigh of relief. I had the deed now. No one could take this business away from me. Sure, I'd had to rely on a handout from my uncle, but from here on out, I'd do all of this myself. I'd make my own destiny without the royal responsibilities telling me what I should want for myself.

There was only one person I wanted to celebrate with. As I stood in the hot afternoon sunshine at the marina, I took my phone out and texted Max.

> Meet me at the marina after your shift? I want to watch the sunset with you in my arms.

I didn't have to wait long for an answer.

> How could I resist the offer? Meet you there soon!

I might have been pushing my luck, but I walked down the pier until I came to Uncle Leo's yacht. With a look left and then right, and seeing no one around to ask what I was doing there, I jumped onboard and got ready for my woman.

Chapter Fifteen
MAXINE

"Where you headed all dolled up like a movie star?" Franny asked me as I checked my lipstick one last time in the mirror in the back room at the diner.

I'd changed into a pair of white eyelet shorts and a tank top, and pulled on some wedge sandals that Bo had delivered for me (after a significant amount of convincing on my part and a final agreement to bring home pie from my next shift.) I doubted movie stars looked much like me, but I appreciated the compliment.

I turned to face her. "Just over to the marina."

Franny's eyebrows went up. "Your fancy friend has a yacht?"

"It's his uncle's, I think."

She nodded knowingly. In high school, the yacht club was the ultimate dividing line between the families on the north and south sides of the island. They had boats. We did not. Or at least not the kind that came with kitchens, bathrooms, and furniture. Bo and I had the Yertle Turtle, but it was just a skiff he used for fishing and riding around.

"Don't get arrested, Max."

I blew out a huff. "We're adults, Franny. I'm hardly sneaking onto someone's boat without their permission."

She looked slightly disappointed, but then nodded. "Oh. Right."

"You on the schedule tomorrow?" I asked her.

"I always work Thursday."

For a brief second, I let the strange panic I'd been feeling about my dwindling hours rise up again, but I pushed it down. "Thought I did too. But I'm not on tomorrow."

Franny frowned at me, and then turned to the paper schedule pinned to the bulletin board. "Huh," she said. "They put Sandy and then Al. What'd you do to piss off Arlene?"

I shook my head. Arlene and her husband Buzz had given me the job at the diner when I'd first graduated school, back when Aunt Glenda watched Bo in the afternoons and I had just a few hours a day to try to cobble together a life for us. I'd been here as long as I could rationally remember, and the idea of losing this job wasn't one I liked to contemplate, though I'd fantasized about leaving the waitressing life many times. "I have no idea."

Arlene and Buzz were rarely at the diner in person anymore. They were both aging and ill, but Arlene had been putting the schedule together every Sunday since the day I started. And she wasn't a fan of change.

Something was wrong, but I wasn't going to dig into it right then. I had a man to meet on a fancy yacht at the marina for sunset.

"Well, if you hear anything, let me know," I told Franny. "But I guess I'll see you Friday."

She gave me a quick hug. "Have fun, honey."

I picked up the cheeseburgers I'd ordered at the end of my shift and headed out, parking just outside the marina parking lot gates and checking my lipstick one more time. Butterflies swirled inside my stomach as I thought of Cav, waiting for me on Leo's enormous yacht.

I squared my shoulders and walked through the front gates, the man in the little booth waving me through with a smile and not a single question.

Following the path through the manicured shrubs toward the Yacht Club, I had a refreshing feeling of belonging here. After all these years, maybe none of this north end, south end stuff really mattered. We were all just people, afterall. But it felt nice to pretend to be a northender for a bit.

"Psst!"

I'd turned down the ramp toward the docks where all the enormous white boats bobbed in the fading sunlight, and an exaggerated whisper floated toward me again.

"Max! Duck down a bit!"

I looked to my left to see Cav on the back of one of the biggest yachts in the marina, comically squatting down as if he were hiding from something looming over us.

I glanced around, but didn't see any reason to duck. There wasn't another soul around. I sped up a bit, coming to stand in front of where Cav hovered at the front of Leo's boat.

"Hey Prince Cav," I said. His hair was catching the orange rays of the sun and he looked more handsome than ever. "Permission to board?"

I handed him the burgers, and then he helped me onto the boat, pulling me toward the bow, which faced the open water to the east and south. To the west lay the yacht club, and as I looked back, I could see the patio to the restaurant full of people enjoying the late afternoon sun.

Cav pulled me down onto a pile of pillows and blankets he'd arranged in the center of the bow between the benches that ran along the sides of the boat. "You look beautiful," he said, coming to sit at my side and looking at me with such warmth in his eyes it sent my heart into a rapid rhythm that made me a little breathless.

"This is cozy," I told him, a bit confused why we didn't just sit on the little benches, or go inside and use actual furniture. But I imagined Cav was trying to make it romantic, and he hadn't failed there.

He pulled the brown paper bag to his lap and inhaled. "This smells heavenly," he said. "Think it will pair with this?" He reached to one side and retrieved an ice bucket with a bottle of champagne chilling inside.

"I think cheeseburgers and champagne are one of the classic pairings," I told him.

Soon, we were leaning back, side by side, sipping champagne as Cav finished the few fries I hadn't demolished myself. "I really need to learn how to make these at home once I have my apartment set up," Cav said.

"Oh, no. They'll never be as good," I told him.

"You don't have faith in my cooking skills?" He frowned at me.

"It's not that. But it's a well-established fact that fries always taste best out of a greasy diner kitchen. Just can't repli-

THE SPARE AND THE SINGLE MOM

cate it at home." I sipped my champagne. "Can you cook, Cav?"

His brows pulled together. "No, not really." His eyes drifted toward the darkening horizon. "Maybe I can. I've just never really had the chance."

I was about to ask Cav more about how he grew up, what kind of life he'd had as a boy, but he'd turned to me and was gazing into my eyes, sending my insides fluttering again.

"I'm so glad I met you," he said. He lifted one hand to cup my cheek, and my skin heated as I leaned into the touch.

"Me too," I said, my voice barely a breath.

The sun was sinking behind the building at our backs, and the air around us took on a thicker, quieter quality as Cav leaned in to press his lips to mine.

I slipped my arms around him, leaning back into the pillows and blankets where we sat, and enjoying the solid weight of him over me, the rush of his lips on my throat, his hands sliding along my sides. The kiss intensified, and I pressed up into him, wanting more, wanting to feel him everywhere.

Soon, he straddled me, and rose up to look down into my face, both our chests heaving with effort and desire. "God, you're a beautiful woman." His voice was reverent, and for a long moment I felt worshiped, cared for. I let the feeling wash through me, pushing out the lingering insecurities that came with a life of never being quite good enough.

I reached for him, pulling him down to me and arching my body beneath his as his lips met mine again, soft and demanding at once.

Lights twinkled to life around us as true darkness washed across the moonless sky, and it was like no one else existed in the world but me and Cav. The sounds of our breaths mingled with the water lapping against the sides of the big boats tied up all around us, and the rocking motion of the deck pushed away the thoughts warring for prominence in my mind. Thoughts suggesting this wasn't a good idea, telling me I didn't know this man.

But what difference did it make? I'd known Bo's dad well. And look how that had ended.

I surrendered my mind to sensation, and soon my hands were pulling at the button on Cav's jeans. We sat up for a moment, our eyes meeting. And then, without a word, we each pulled off clothing. Cav slipped his jeans off, revealing a nearly perfect ass clad only in a pair of dark green boxer briefs, and I pulled my tank top off over my head.

Cav took my mouth again, his body following mine to the soft blankets under us, and I let my hands wander over the smooth hard muscles of his back, the firm round globes of his ass. And finally, I chanced letting one hand slide around his body and pressed my palm to the significant length I felt pressed to my hip.

"Oh god," he murmured against my throat where he was dropping kisses and nipping softly in a way that was driving me toward the edge, making me feel reckless.

He was hard and thick, and as soon as my fingers wrapped the girth of him, I wanted more. I wanted it all.

"Do you have a condom?" I asked him.

He paused, pressing himself up to look into my face, concern written there in the dark cast of his eyes, the lowered brows. "I do. Are you sure–"

I didn't let him finish the question. I'd never been more sure

THE SPARE AND THE SINGLE MOM

of anything. It might be a mistake, but I didn't care. And I honestly didn't think it was. Cav was a gentleman. He was respectful and sweet, and I was going to let myself enjoy him. All of him.

Soon enough, there was nothing between us but the night air, and Cav reached for his jeans to retrieve the condom. I watched the way the muscles of his torso rippled as he moved, the dim twinkling lights around us catching the planes and ridges of muscle.

He sheathed himself, and rolled to one hip, leaving his leg intertwined with mine, but freeing up a hand to skate down my body, lingering on the skin of my belly as he kissed me again. And then, as he deepened the kiss, his fingers teased lower.

"Oh!" I breathed when the thick rounds of his fingertips played across my sensitive flesh. "Oh, Cav." His fingers danced and teased, delving into the wetness I felt between my legs and back out, rubbing in the right places, tracing lightly around others.

It was driving me mad. Every time his fingers landed right where I wanted them, he'd work me into a frenzy until my body was writhing and twitching at his touch, and then he'd back off.

I heard myself whimpering, practically pleading with him as all rational thought was chased away by desire, and finally, his hand returned with perfect pressure right where I needed it.

"Oh, god. Oh, yes... right theeeere," I heard myself moan.

Cav took my mouth again as his fingers worked a demanding rhythm, pushing me closer and closer to a release I could already tell might just kill me. But it was too late to stop it, too late to do anything. My body had taken over, and the rest of me was just standing by to see how it all ended.

I reached for Cav, needing more, needing something. "I want..." I managed to say.

"I've got you, Max," he whispered in my ear, his voice thick and husky. And a second later, I felt him notched against me, the satisfying thickness of him pressing into me, moving slowly right where I needed him.

"I don't..." I wasn't sure what I meant to say, but when Cav pressed farther inside me, words failed me entirely.

"God, Max. Oh god," he whispered, his mouth against my ear as he filled me in the most delicious way possible, every nerve inside me alight with sensation and need.

When he was fully seated, he lingered there, both of us breathing heavily, the motion of the boat doing half the work for us as we rocked gently together. I clung to him like a lifeline, the rest of my body and mind fully out of my own control at that point, everything in me focused on the delicious fullness of having Cav inside me.

He began to move, slowly at first, and then more determinedly, my hips arching up to meet him with every thrust as I edged ever closer to oblivion.

For a second, I popped my eyes open, and that was the beginning of the end. Cav labored over me, that lock of dark hair flopping into his face as his forehead creased with concentration. His eyes held mine, and there was something so tender there, so open and unguarded, that it sent me straight off the cliff.

"Oh!" I managed, just as my body took control, shuddering and pulsing around Cav's delicious cock. The orgasm raced through me, from my toes through my stomach, filling my vision with stars before concentrating right at my center, in the spot where we were connected.

Cav seemed to wait for me, and then he groaned, low and husky. "So beautiful," he heaved, and then I felt his orgasm overtake him. His strong body flexed and went rigid beneath my hands, and he groaned again, long and low, before collapsing onto me. "My god, woman. You nearly killed me," he whispered into my ear.

I smiled, staring up into the night sky where the stars had just begun to pop through the dusky heavens above. My hands traced lines up and down Cav's back as a strange fulfillment filled me. Soon though, Cav's weight became too much.

"Cav, I can barely breathe."

"Oh, sorry." He rolled to one side, and for a moment, my body mourned the loss of him. I snuggled closer.

"That was..."

"Amazing," he said, staring intently into my face. "You are amazing."

I kissed him then, feeling freer than I had in years. "You're okay, yourself, Prince."

He frowned. "I wish you wouldn't call me that."

"Why?"

His eyes lifted to the sky and then returned to my face. "It just feels wrong now, that's all."

"Okay."

We lay there like that, both of us looking up into the sky, for a long time. Finally, Cav turned to me and I felt his eyes on the side of my face.

"Can I ask a question? You don't have to answer it."

"Sure, you can ask," I said. I was so relaxed, I didn't think there was anything he could ask that would disturb me.

"What happened to Bo's dad? Is he involved in his life at all?"

A little tension crept back into my body, and I sighed. "He's not." I knew he wanted more, so I made myself talk about the thing I rarely discussed. "He was my high school boyfriend. But it was a classic case of star-crossed lovers, I guess. I was from the wrong side of town. His family didn't really approve of me. And when I got pregnant... that was the end of it."

"Did you tell him?"

I laughed. "Yeah. But he had a football scholarship and plans to leave the little town we grew up in and never come back."

"Is that what he did?"

"Pretty much."

"He knew he had a child, and he's never so much as come back to meet him?"

It hurt to think about, but I rolled to face Cav, scanning the handsome face as if I could reassure myself that I could trust this man. "He came back once. Right after college. Bo was four."

"And what happened?"

I'd been so stupid. So hopeful. "I let him take us out to dinner. Let myself believe he'd come back to do the right thing, to know his son."

Cav pulled me closer. "That wasn't what happened."

I shook my head. "He bought us dinner. Then he asked me to sign a bunch of papers his father had given him."

"Papers?"

"Saying I'd never ask him for any financial support, that I relinquished any claim to his family's money."

"Did you sign?"

I pushed away from Cav, feeling the hurt all over again. "I signed. I didn't want his money. I wanted everything else. A chance for a normal life for my son. A family to call his own." I squeezed my eyes shut. I was not going to shed any more tears over this, no matter how new the hurt felt as I told Cav everything. "My parents kicked me out, and they never wanted to meet their grandson. We had my aunt, and that was it. I wanted more for Bo."

"Oh darling," Cav pulled me close, ignoring the stiffness in my limbs, the resistance I put up at first. After a moment I relaxed into him. "You've given your son such a good life, Max. All by yourself. You should be very proud."

I let the words soak in. I'd been on my own so long, I'd forgotten what that kind of approval felt like. I hugged Cav back, letting happiness replace the bad memories, the feelings of never belonging.

"Hey!" A voice came from the dock next to the boat just as a flashlight beam landed on us. Cav quickly pulled a blanket up to cover me. "Hey, what are you doing on there?"

Cav sat up, looking suddenly very authoritative, even regal. "We are enjoying our yacht, sir, and I'd thank you to lower your beam."

"Well, there's just a couple problems there, sir," the man said, his southern twang making the word 'sir' sound like a slur. "This here's Leo Barclay's yacht, and I'm pretty sure you ain't him."

"Leo Barclay is my uncle," Cav said indignantly.

"You got a letter of permission from Uncle Leo?" the man asked, sounding smug.

"I...Well..."

"Y'all better skedaddle. I'm gonna head on over to that booth back there and make a quick call to security. Maybe they'll find an empty boat. Or maybe they'll be inviting a couple scalawags to spend the night in the local jail. Up to you." The flashlight beam left us, making the night seem darker than it had before.

I pulled my clothes on quickly as Cav dressed and then gathered the blankets in his arms. "Do you mind grabbing the—"

But I'd already collected our trash and jumped onto the dock, shoving the paper bag into a nearby garbage can. Up ahead, we could see the lights of a security vehicle drawing closer to the marina.

"Run!" Cav suggested, and I didn't ask questions. We hustled out of the marina, out the front gate of the club and dove into my car, which I drove away from the yacht club like a woman possessed. "I guess I'll sneak back over tomorrow to get my truck," Cav said.

When we'd finally gotten back to the southern end of the island, I pulled over and glared at him. "We didn't have permission to use your uncle's boat?"

He shook his head. "I'm so sorry, Max. I should've—"

But I was already laughing.

"What?"

"It's just..." I caught my breath and faced him. "I've spent my whole life coming from the wrong side of town, the wrong side of the island. And then I met the most proper, fancy guy

I've ever encountered. I guess some tiny part of me thought everything would be different with you, but here we are, still running from the cops!" I watched as Cav's face broke into a smile and he chuckled. But he didn't look happy.

"You deserve better," he said, the smile falling altogether.

"It's fine," I assured him.

"No," he said, straightening up. "It's not fine. You deserve to be treated like a queen." In a much softer voice, he added, "you deserve the truth."

I wasn't sure what he meant by that, but I didn't ask. Because when I pulled up in front of Cav's property, both our jaws dropped open in shock. His land had been turned into a parking lot...for Walmart shopping carts.

"There must be at least a hundred of them," I surmised.

"Maybe closer to five hundred," Cav said, sounding impressed.

We turned to look at one another. "Angus."

Chapter Sixteen
FIONA

> Do you really love him so much you'll throw your life away to join him in America?

I reread the message I'd received from the Queen this morning. She really was clueless as to what was going on here. Cavanaugh and I had never been in love, though that fact hadn't mattered in their plans for us. I knew what I wanted to text her back with, but had a feeling she wouldn't appreciate me talking about her son's balls.

> The spare finally grew a pair, my Queen.

I laughed out loud at my own crude joke, pulled up the handle on my suitcase, and wheeled it out of the hotel room I'd been checked out of for failing my mission for the crown. North Carolina was already changing me in ways I had yet to comprehend. For example, I traded my pair of heels for a sensible ballet flat today. I felt like everyone was staring at me as I left the hotel. Could ballet flats really be so scandalously casual? Or was it the non-name brand blouse that was already sticking to my skin as I squinted into the morning sun and debated my options?

I needed to warn Cavanaugh that the Queen was aware of my failure and would most likely send reinforcements to get the job done. He needed to prepare for a confrontation. His time was up.

I also needed to find a place to live. My own parents would be hearing from the Queen soon, which would lead to incessant messages from them, mostly in the form of harassment about coming home and finding another marriage match to save our family name.

But they didn't understand either. Despite my intentions, Sailfish Banks had become home. The excitement stamped all over Cavanaugh's face while he explained his plans had somehow infected me with the same "devil may care" attitude. I sucked in a deep breath of warm, humid air and flagged down a taxi cab waiting in a line at the curb of the hotel. The black sedan that had carried me to every destination I needed was no longer idling at the curb at the ready. I needed transportation to Cavanaugh's new place before my parents shut down my personal credit cards. I frowned, sliding into the back of the cab while the driver rolled his eyes and then hefted my suitcase into the trunk himself. A grown woman should have her own credit cards, a belief I did not hold a mere week ago. Now that I was most likely going to be cut off from my parents' finances, I saw things with new eyes.

The spare had indeed grown a pair...and now I needed to also.

I grinned through the window as the trees flickered by. The sparkling ocean peeked out from behind the sand dunes. Life had changed and so had I. Fiona Bettencourt was about to get a job and stand on her own two feet–minus the heels.

Chapter Seventeen
CAVANAUGH

I'd never met a woman like Maxine Waddell. Every woman I'd ever met would have been angry at me for sneaking us onto a boat I didn't have permission to use and then getting caught. They'd have yelled at me, maybe slapped my face, and surely never spoken to me again, but not Max. She thought our little encounter with the security guard was funny. I'd convinced her to sleep with me on an essentially stolen boat, got chased by boat cops, and she was still smiling. Unbelievable.

I wanted to marry this woman. Tie her to my person and never let her go. I definitely wanted to tell her the truth about my family, trusting finally that someone wouldn't hold my heritage against me–or care more about it than who I really was. Max would appreciate me for more than my title, of that I was now sure.

But I couldn't do any of that right then because not only did I have half of Walmart's shopping carts on my property, but

Bo was sitting on my doorstep, a frown on his face that told me he didn't miss the way Max's hair was decidedly mussed.

"Serves you right, dickhead!" Angus's croaking voice echoed across the road. I turned to see him standing in the middle of the dead grass dick-shape that was his front yard.

"Excuse me?" I hollered back, feigning innocence.

Angus shook his fist in the air. "I know you did this, dickhead!"

"I've never been called something so rude," I whispered to Max. She laughed, wiping her eyes.

"Well, if you draw the dick, you get called a dick," she managed to wheeze.

"Is that some sort of North Carolina law?" I asked, knowing full well it wasn't.

The question only made Max laugh harder, which was my intention. Her laughter was music to my ears. And it held off the confrontation I knew I was about to have with her son. Angus spun on his heel and stomped back into his house. Securing Max's hand in mine, I turned to Bo sitting in the weak light from the outside bulb that still worked after all these years of abandonment.

"Any chance you want to help me round up all these carts?"

His gaze dropped to our hands and he stood, pulling his shoulders back and trying to appear tougher than he was. "Think you and I ought to have a conversation first."

"Bo," Max warned as we walked toward him.

"It's fine, Mom. Just a guy-to-guy chat."

Maxine sighed but gave my hand a squeeze before letting go and heading inside. She gave Bo heavy side-eye as she passed, but he kept his gaze trained on me. Once the door shut behind her, I held my hands up.

"I know what you're thinking."

"Oh really?" Bo cut me off. He came down a step so we were staring at each other eye to eye. "Looks like you're making my mom laugh harder than I've heard her laugh in years."

I blinked twice, not prepared for the conversation to go that way. "Yes, she does have an amazing laugh, doesn't she?"

Bo clapped me on the shoulder. "Can't say it's easy to watch this happen. It's my mom, you know? But I'm happy if she's happy. Just make sure you use protection. I don't need a little brother at this point."

I had to fight to close my mouth. I nodded, feeling so awkward I was willing to hightail it to Angus's house and chance being called a dickhead again. "Will do."

Bo moved toward the shopping cart nearest us, pausing with his hands on the push bar. "You better not break her heart or I'll break your legs, Cav. Fancy accent or no accent. Money or not. Don't mess with her heart."

Then he got busy pushing the carts together, the noise drowning out anything I could have responded with. He had a very good point though. I had strong feelings for Max and I knew she returned them. I needed to tell her the truth before this went any further.

I climbed the two stairs and entered the building. "Max?"

"I'm upstairs!"

My blood heated, envisioning all kinds of ways I wanted to hear her say something like that for years to come. Preferably once I had furniture and when her son wasn't right outside the door. I bounded up the stairs and found her spinning in a slow circle.

"What are you doing?" I came up behind her and pulled her into my front, wrapping my arms around her waist and breathing her in. She snuggled into me and all felt right in my world.

"Just envisioning the furniture we picked out. I think the bed should go here. That way you have a view of the trees when you wake up." She pointed to the far wall with an unobstructed view out the window.

"I agree. But let's change that to when *we* wake up."

Max pulled away from me and turned to look up at me. "Cav," she chided. "I have my own house. And Bo. As much as waking up here with you sounds amazing, I can't see that happening."

I left my entire life to start over here. I knew as well as anyone that with enough conviction our lives could change overnight. "Never say never, muscles." I reached down and held her hand. "Do you have time to talk?"

She eyed me wearily. "What did Bo say?"

I grinned. "Not sure you want to hear all of it, but basically he gave us his blessing."

Her eyes went wide. "He said that?"

My head tilted right and left. "Essentially." I tugged her over to the sleeping bag I'd been using most nights. We had a seat and I faced her, our legs tucked under us.

"You're scaring me," she whispered. "Please don't say you regret what happened on the boat. I might have to borrow your sledgehammer and demo something."

I lurched back. "So violent, Max." I squeezed her hands.

"No, nothing like that. I only regret we didn't get longer to snooze in each other's arms before we got chased off."

She blew out a breath. "Okay, good."

"It wasn't good, Max. It was amazing. Mind blowing. Life altering."

Her cheeks went pink and I chided myself for not complimenting her more often. "Agreed."

"Which is why I know I need to tell you the truth. It's time. Maybe past time." I sucked in a deep breath for courage and let it all out. "I come from a royal family. A little country called Mardelvia. My father is king and my older brother is the royal heir."

I paused to give her time to process. Max was frozen in place, staring me down. "Your daddy is king. And that makes you...?"

I shrugged. "The spare."

Her eyes closed for a moment and when she opened them, she was back to her normal self. "So why are you here? You can't be here permanently, then. Oh god, you have to go back, don't you?"

"No. No, I promise you, I'm here for good. My parents would like me to come back, but that's not happening. My life is here now. This business I'm building is it for me. This, with you, is everything I want."

Max shook her head, brows furrowing. "But don't you have, like, obligations and royal duties or something?" Max sat up ramrod straight. "Fiona! She was your betrothed!"

I nodded. "Yes, it was an arranged marriage by the crown, but as I've explained previously, neither she nor I will be going through with it."

"So when I called you Prince Cav, that was..."

My mouth tilted up on one side. "Spot on? Yes, yes it was. A little too much, which is why I asked you to stop. I don't feel like a prince any longer and I don't want to ever be one again."

Max leaned closer. "But why? Didn't you have servants and money and fancy clothes and literally anything you wanted?"

"Yes, I had all those things and yet nothing I wanted. I had duties every single hour of every day. My life was under a microscope all the time and the next fifty years were scripted out for me. I want to make my own life, Max. The only way to do that was to move here to America. My parents will be sending someone to bring me back, so expect that, but just know I will not go. My life is here in North Carolina. With you."

Max let go of my hands and jumped to her feet. She paced back and forth in my apartment, muttering under her breath. On her fifth lap around the room, she accidentally kicked one of my duffle bags. A clanking noise drew our eyes to a shiny gold object rolling straight for the wall. I reached out and snatched it up, sliding the bulky ring onto my hand.

"This is our royal crest." I stood up and showed her, letting her take in the crest that had been my family's for innumerable generations before me.

Max tilted her head back and speared me with her blue eyes. "You don't want to go back? Ever?"

I cupped her jaw. "Never. I promise you."

"Okay," she whispered.

I lowered my head and captured her mouth. With Max, it was that simple. She trusted me and I trusted her.

A throat clearing had us breaking apart. Bo stood in the doorway, his gaze averted. "Got all the carts together, but it'll take a truck to haul them back to town." His gaze settled on the heavy ring on my finger but he didn't ask any questions. I wondered how much he might have heard.

"Thanks, Bo. I'll take care of it in the morning." Looking back at Max, I considered the woman I was most definitely in love with. Her acceptance of my background meant the world to me. "Let's walk you to your car."

All three of us traipsed downstairs, Bo taking his mom home in his beat-up sedan. We promised to get together tomorrow when the furniture arrived. I waved them off and went back inside. I saw a pink sticky note on the framed-out bar area downstairs. With a smile, I snatched it up, expecting some sort of insight into Max's brain or heart, but saw messy handwriting that would have made a doctor proud.

I'm not kidding. Sheath the sausage.

I sputtered. Jesus. Bo was as forthright as his mother.

Chapter Eighteen
MAXINE

"What exactly did you say to him, Bo?" I asked my son as he drove me home, his big hands wrapped so tightly around the wheel I worried he might pull it off.

Bo glanced at me, looking fierce and angry, and for a moment I saw my father the night he told me he was disappointed in me and that I'd made my own bed and would have to lie in it. But as I stared at my son, the image slid away, replaced by the face of the strong, responsible boy I'd done my best to raise. My dad was in there, but Bo had soft edges where my father had only sharp points.

"I told him he'd better treat you right or he'd be answering to me," he said. "And I told him to wrap it up when he, ah... you know."

Embarrassment made me sit up straighter. "Bo!" I imagined my tough-guy son, raised in the outer banks of North Carolina in dirt and seawater and sunshine telling a prince from some far-away land to keep his cobra in its sack, and burst into laughter. "Oh my god, you did not!"

"I did," he sniffed. "You deserve the best, Mom. And I'm happy being an only child."

I was still laughing, trying to picture Cav's face as my son discussed his sex life with him.

We pulled into the driveway and Bo looked at me with a mixture of amusement and hurt in his eyes. "You laughing at me, Mom?" For a second, I saw the sweet little boy he'd been, his blond curls falling in those honest blue eyes of his.

"No, honey," I managed, pulling myself together and taking a deep breath. "Thank you for looking out for me. I appreciate that. A lot." I touched his cheek and smiled at him as my heart thumped inside my chest. I wasn't sure how much more it could take in one day. "I'm laughing because I was picturing you talking to Cav that way. And because he told me something that makes it particularly funny that you were telling him to keep his hose housed."

Bo made a face at my expression. I could have gone on for hours with euphemisms like that, but this wasn't the time.

"Cav told me tonight that he's actually a prince. From some far away kingdom. That he came here to escape his royal duties and make a life for himself."

"And you believed him?" Bo's expression shuttered. "That dirty creep..."

"Yes, I believe him."

"Mom. Come on."

I shook my head, waiting for Bo to continue.

"He's making that up. To get in your pants."

I hadn't thought about that before, but now that I did, I

knew with certainty it wasn't true. "I doubt anyone would be that desperate to get with me, Bo. Plus, it's not like he's after our money, right? Since we don't have any and all..."

"I guess, but..."

"I believe him. And Fiona showing up just gives more validation to the story."

"Fiona?"

"His fiancee." I almost choked at Bo's angry expression. "Former fiancee. I mean, not really. Hey, do you suppose we could go inside?" I pushed open my door and got out of the sedan. "And tomorrow could you take me back over to get my car?"

"Don't you have to be at work?"

I shook my head, the worry I'd been pushing away finally jumping back to mind. "No. I've only got about half my usual shifts this week. It's so weird."

"Okay," Bo said, ignoring my concern and following me into the house. "You sure you're okay? You trust this guy?" Bo faced me in our little living room, worry creasing his face.

I reached up and laid a hand on his cheek. "I do, honey. Don't you?"

He let out a breath and then smiled. "Yeah. I do. I just want to protect you."

"And I love you for it."

I watched my son head down the hall and close his door and then flopped down on the couch to replay the events of what had turned into the best day of my life.

I was in love with Cav. I had no doubt about it. And the fact that he was a prince? It was crazy, but I found it didn't matter one little bit. Except in one very important way. Even up against servants and money and anything he could ever need... he was choosing me.

He was choosing me - something no one else had ever done. Not my family, not Bo's dad. And now, apparently not Arlene at the diner. But Cav chose me, and it lit up a dark place inside me that had me unworried about all the other little irritations in my life.

The next day, Bo dropped me off at Cav's and then headed to school. The days were getting longer and hotter, and my little boy was only weeks from graduation. It was hard to believe.

"Hey beautiful," Cav said, stepping out his front door. I was about to answer when someone stepped out behind him.

Fiona.

She wore silk pajamas and her hair was tied up in some kind of silky helmet that I felt like I might have seen once on an old episode of "I Love Lucy."

Why was Fiona here? Jealousy threatened to erupt in my stomach, but Cav stepped down the stairs and wrapped me in an embrace before I could process my concern. And then he was kissing me so lovingly, so resoundingly, that any jealousy was immediately banished. You didn't kiss someone like that if you were sleeping with the pajama-clad woman behind you and trying to be sly about it.

"Hi," I managed when he let me go, putting a hand to my own hair and trying to find my wits again.

"Good morning," Fiona said, sounding far too proper for a

woman standing on a half-demolished property filled with tractors and cinder blocks.

"Hey there," I answered, and the three of us stepped back inside.

The bar had been laid out, and the windows were all in, trimmed out and looking somewhat finished. I hadn't even noticed it all the night before, I'd been so flushed after everything with Cav. The place was looking good.

"Fiona is going to be staying down here for a bit," Cav said.

"The jig, as they say, is up," she confirmed. "The crown has cut me off and my parents did the same when I told them I would not be coming home to be subjected to yet another loveless match that would only benefit our family name."

"Damn right," I said, raising my hand to give her a high five.

Fiona stared at my raised hand, her eyebrows raised in surprise. I reached down and took her hand, showing her how to slap mine. "High five."

"Oh." She nodded.

"Max, could I have a word?" Cav asked, standing on the stairs at the back of the space.

"Sure," I said, and followed him up. "What time does the furniture get here?" I asked.

"Ten, I think," he said, reaching into the closet for something. He popped back out with a rose in his hand that looked suspiciously like those growing next door in Edith's garden. "This is for you."

"Thank you," I said. "That's sweet."

The look he gave me then wasn't sweet at all. It was downright predatory, and he took my jaw in his palm and moved closer, sending heat rushing through me.

"You," he whispered, his voice sounding strained as he pulled me close to him, "are driving me insane. You're all I can think about. Especially after last night." He touched his lips to mine then, moving away too quickly for my liking.

My arms went around him, and things started tingling as I remembered being on the boat with him, in his arms, the way he'd moved in me. I could feel the heat of him pressed to my hip, hard and firm.

"Max," he said. "I need to tell you something."

I froze. Was this it? The part where he told me he wasn't choosing me after all? I braced myself for it.

"I love you," he whispered, touching his forehead to mine. "I've fallen in love with you."

Glee and relief chased one another through my chest, and happiness made me feel like I was suddenly standing beneath a rainbow disco ball, Cav and I alone at the center of the universe's very best dance party.

"You do?" I asked, wanting to make sure.

"I do," he said, smiling down at me.

"Good. Because I fell in love with you pretty much the first time you opened your mouth."

"No you did not. You hated me."

"You were annoying. That doesn't mean I didn't want you."

"Oh, you wanted me, Max?" He pressed against me more firmly, grinning.

"I did. And I do. And I love you too, Prince Cav."

"But not because of my title."

I frowned at him. "You don't really think that, do you?"

"Just checking."

I laughed and pressed myself against his steely warmth. "I love you too," I whispered, and then he kissed me, long and hard, and full of promises.

"Excuse me, your highness," Fiona called up. "Oh! I mean, no! I didn't mean to say... that is, uh, Cavanaugh, sir. Oh no."

We headed down the stairs as Fiona continued backpedaling, digging a deeper and deeper hole. She looked at Cav with huge apologetic eyes.

"I'm so sorry."

"I already told her about my family, Fi. It's fine."

"Oh thank goodness." She let out a huge breath, and turned to point to the front lawn. "The furniture seems to have arrived."

Indeed, a huge truck was parked out front and a couple men were unloading a couch.

"Let's help them figure out where to put everything," I suggested. "Hey, is Ben coming out today?"

Cav shook his head. "No, but he gave some of Cyrus's men instructions yesterday, and they're going to lay the pads for the tiny houses today."

"Great," I said, pulling open the front door as an idea occurred to me. "Hey, Fiona, you're sticking around then?"

"I am," she said.

"And so... you've met Ben?"

She frowned and looked at Cav. "No, why?"

Cav looked at me questioningly and then a slow smile began to spread across his sculpted lips. "Are you matchmaking, Maxine?"

"No, just thinking."

He winked. "Good idea." He looked at Fiona as we stepped outside to meet the furniture movers. "It's inevitable that you'll meet Ben soon. He's here all the time."

Fiona looked slightly uncomfortable with the conversation, so I let it drop, moving to help direct furniture into the apartment.

"Bed first," I suggested. "We're gonna need it."

Chapter Nineteen
CAVANAUGH

As the delivery guys brought each piece into the apartment, I told them where to put it and Max had them move it. Each time, she was right. It always looked better where she suggested, quite like all the renovations. It hadn't escaped my notice that she'd been coming behind me all along and fixing the little things I got wrong. Who knew you needed to tape drywall seams before you mudded them? Or that flooring had to go in before the baseboards? None of that had been in my royal training program. Ask me to fence and I was your guy. Ask me to lay flooring and you'd be better served talking to Max. It made me sad that so much of my training was actually useless in the real world.

When the delivery guys had left and Fiona was busy downstairs measuring exactly where each appliance and barstool would go before she went shopping with the last of the cash I had on hand, Max helped me unpack my duffle bags, placing my limited amount of clothing in the new dresser drawers. She held up my family ring, sliding it onto her finger and prancing about the apartment like she had imaginary heels on her bare feet. The gold ring looked absolutely massive on her small hand.

"Oh peasant boy, would you wash my feet?" she simpered in some ridiculous accent I couldn't place. Literally no one talked like that, not even a prince from a royal family.

I came over and held her hand, bowing at the waist to kiss her knuckles. If she wanted to play, I would oblige her. There was nothing I loved more than seeing Max smile. "M'lady, perhaps there is a more pressing matter at hand."

Max lifted an eyebrow. "Oh, and what is that?"

I tilted my head toward the new bed, complete with the new sheet and comforter set I'd picked up in a bargain bin at WalMart. That place had everything, indeed. "This bed must be broken in before m'lady can sleep in it."

"Broken in?" she broke character, dropping that terrible accent.

My wagging eyebrows told her what my mouth didn't. Her eyes lit up and she let out a squeal when I picked her up and deposited her on top of the bed with a bounce. "Stay quiet, m'lady."

I dropped to my knees and stripped the jean shorts off her legs, which tugged her closer to the edge of the bed. Placing her thighs over my shoulders, I let my fingers trace across the simple strip of black lace that separated her flesh from mine. My woman was already wet for me.

"Cav!" she whisper-shouted.

"Hush, m'lady. One more noise from you and we will get caught."

My finger dove beneath the edge of the lace and Max gasped, then grabbed one of the pillows off the bed to press to her face. I swallowed back a smile and moved the lace to the side. I needed to taste her. Needed to feel her tightening around me again. Needed to know that she was mine, even with a rough comforter beneath her soft skin, knowing I couldn't provide her with more. At least not yet.

I dove right in, my tongue sweeping across her flesh. Her back bowed off the bed, but my palm held her down while my other hand kept her panties out of the way. Her scent surrounded me, transporting me to a world in which this was my whole life. Her and me and this old building, eking out a life that we'd chosen together. Her muffled cries above me urged me on. I sucked that bundle of nerves that made her wild into my mouth, a single finger sliding into her heat. She fell apart quickly, the quivering of her thighs and the pulsing flesh around my finger bringing a sense of satisfaction that had nothing to do with my aching dick. I wanted to give Max everything. She believed in us and that meant everything to me.

As she came down I gazed at her hands gripping the pillow to her face, my family crest sparkling in the sunlight. I'd never looked at that ring and felt satisfaction, only obligation, yet Max had given it new life. I'd always appreciate where I came from, but Max and this town were my future.

"Good girl, m'lady," I whispered, getting to my feet and pulling her from the bed. "You may have your shorts back now for being so quiet."

Max threw the pillow back on the bed and scrambled to her feet, her cheeks bright red and her golden hair a mess around her face. Her eyes sparkled and her chest heaved as she tried to catch her breath. I liked this look on her. She slid the ring off her finger and handed it to me before pulling on her shorts.

"I'll be careful next time I put on that ring if that's the result," she finally muttered under her breath.

I chuckled as I moved away to put the ring in the back of the top drawer of the dresser. "I thought I heard Cyrus's truck pull up, but your thighs were squeezing my head so tightly I might be wrong."

"Oh my god, Cav!" Max was back to whisper-shouting. "Do you think they heard?"

I didn't care if they did, but I had a feeling that wasn't the answer she was looking for. "No, of course not. You were very quiet." I pointed to her hair. "But you might want to fix your hair before we go downstairs."

Her hands pawed at her hair and I tried not to laugh. She was adorable. And mine.

Cyrus was indeed downstairs with most of his crew. He took one look at Max and shot me a glare. I held my hands up and he shook his head. He started barking orders and the crew got to work on finishing the long wooden bar that would be the centerpiece of this place. Fiona had a pen in her hair and a list in her hands that she was studying. I'd never seen her look so casual, but it looked good on her.

"I can help carry in the bartop," I told Cyrus, wanting to help.

The man screeched to a halt in his heavy work boots and looked to Max for help. "Uh, yeah, thanks, Cav, but I think we got it. I think you and Max had plans?"

Max looked back and forth between us several times before she jerked to attention. "Oh, yeah. Those plans." She turned to me. "How do you feel about fishing?"

I narrowed my eyes. "Are you trying to get rid of me?"

Max's eyes went wide, but Cyrus was the one who answered. "Yep. Sure are, boss. You have great vision, but your construction skills are lacking. We'll get more done with you gone."

I stood up straight and gave Cyrus a look I'd seen my mother give to anyone who dared cross her. "I shall remember this, Cyrus."

Unlike my mother's subjects, Cyrus just snorted, completely unaffected. "If you think about it, maybe bring me back some coffee when you're done with your plans?"

I opened my mouth to give him some blistering advice about how to treat paying clients, but Max cut me off and shoved me out the door. "Sounds good, have fun!"

"You don't get seasick, do you?" she asked me, clearly trying to change the subject.

I pouted. "I can hammer things. Dig things. I can even drywall."

Max shot me a look over the top of her sedan. "Really, Cav? You missed every single stud."

I tried not to let my feelings be hurt. "Not my fault really. Studs are eighteen on-center in my country." I'd read that online, but much after the fact.

Max scoffed, but when we climbed in her car, she ran her hand up and down my arm. "Listen, let's just let the professionals do their jobs and we'll go catch dinner on the Yertle Turtle."

"The what?"

Max laughed and pulled the car out onto the road. "You'll see."

Calling this contraption below my feet a boat was very generous. I could see more patches than smooth metal. The tiny motor on the back had belched out black smoke before settling into a steady hum as Max puttered us out into a shallow alcove along the barrier island, south of Sailfish Banks. She assured me that this was where she and Bo had caught fish without even trying.

She handed me a pole and looked quite impressed when I baited my own line and tossed it in the water without detailed instructions.

"I visited my Uncle Leo a few summers growing up, you know," I said dryly.

She winced. "Sorry. I just figured you didn't get to do much fishing as a prince."

I shook my head, staring out at the fairly placid water, each little ripple sparkling like a thousand tiny diamonds in the sunshine. I could feel the stress I carried about my family and my future melting away with each gentle rock of the boat. "I ate a lot of fish as a prince, but no. My parents didn't let us catch it ourselves. Our loss, really."

Max settled on the bench next to me, her line on the opposite side of the boat. "When being a single parent got to be too much, I'd always take Bo fishing. Nothing like sitting around for hours staring at the water to let your mind settle."

I nudged her shoulder. "You're not alone anymore, muscles."

To my horror, her eyes filled with tears, one side spilling

over onto her cheek. I set the pole in the bottom of the boat and wrapped my arms around her. "I didn't mean to make you cry, love."

She shook her head, more tears spilling over. "It's happy crying."

I kissed the top of her head. Women were strange creatures. I opened my mouth to say something–anything–to get her to stop crying, but my pole slid violently across the bottom of the boat. With a shout, I grabbed the pole in my hands, feeling that telltale tugging at the end of the line. I leaped to my feet and the boat began to rock dangerously. Max yelled something and the fish on my line tugged harder. We nearly went overboard, but somehow managed to stay in the little boat and reel in my fish. Max took a picture of me holding up the flopping tarpon, a wide grin on my face.

I forgot about my family back home and simply let myself enjoy the summer day with the woman I loved.

Chapter Twenty
MAXINE

I would not have predicted it in a million years, but Prince Cav was actually a great fisherman. A natural, even. He didn't flinch at baiting the line, cleaning his catch, or the idea of eating our haul.

And we did eat it. Most of it, anyway. We took it back to my house, and when Bo came home he had Gator and Colby in tow. Luckily there was plenty of tarpon to go around, and when we were done, the strangest feeling came over me. I looked to where Cav sat, a satisfied grin on his face as he finished his plate, and then let my gaze drift to my handsome son, and the friends he'd had since kindergarten.

Life was good. My life, for once, was good.

"How're things at home, Gator?" I knew he'd had a tough stretch recently. His parents weren't exactly model citizens, and from what Bo said, Gator was raising his little sister on his own.

"Dad left again," he said, in the same voice you'd use to tell someone it looked like rain. "And Mom's been high since at least March." He shrugged.

Man, I hadn't given Bo much, but at least I was here. Sober. Doing what I could.

"I'm sorry, son."

Gator caught my eye then, and the look I saw on his face nearly broke my heart. His eyes warred in his face, pulling back and forth between little boy tears and righteous teen anger. "Nothin' to be sorry about." His chin jutted and I sensed it would be best to leave that alone.

"Well," Cav said, clearly sensing that this was a good point at which to clear the table and move on with the evening. "Let's get these dishes handled." I watched as the prince of some country I'd never heard of cleared my table and carried dishes to the sink, rolling up his sleeves for the task.

Bo stood and moved in next to him. "Sir, we have a rule in these parts. You catch 'em, you don't clean."

Cav turned to my son with a wide smile. "You sure?"

"Yes sir. C'mon Colby. A hand?"

Cav returned to his seat by my side and we leaned into one another as the boys cleaned up. The warmth radiating off Cav's body assured me that I might not have a palace or a crown, but I had enough.

Soon, the boys headed out for the evening, and I convinced Cav to watch reruns of *Murder, She Wrote* with me on the couch.

"How is it that one middle aged woman in a tiny town on the coast finds herself involved in so many murders?" he asked, raising a point I'd often pondered. "If there were that many murders in your town, wouldn't you think about moving?"

I laughed, loving the strong firmness of his chest beneath my head, the way his arm felt around my shoulder.

When I asked the prince to stay over, he agreed easily, and we spent the remainder of the night alternately laughing and moaning in ecstasy. And when we finally drifted to sleep, I did so in the circle of Cav's strong arms, wondering how I'd ever gotten so lucky.

The next morning, Cav, Bo, and I headed to Cav's place to check the new pads scattered around the property for the tiny houses, and to see what Fiona had been up to in the bar. Cav had agreed to let her decorate the place, and when we walked in, it looked more like something that belonged on *Downton Abbey* than in Sailfish Banks.

"This is the fanciest dive bar I've ever seen," Bo said, looking around at the heavy draperies and crystal chandeliers.

"How many dive bars have you seen?" I asked suspiciously.

"Uh, none," he answered.

"Good answer," Cav said.

"Did you still want me to check the sink up there?" Bo asked, pointing toward the stairs. He'd come with us this morning because Cav had told him he hadn't been quite sure that he'd tightened the supply lines right for the sink in the upstairs bath.

"If you don't mind," Cav said.

"Not at all," Bo said, heading up the stairs.

"Fiona, we might need to discuss decor," Cav said, looking at his friend.

She sniffed, passing a hand fondly over the tufted chair cushions on the chairs scattered around antique tables. "You'd like to tell me I did a good job, I assume?"

"Um. Yes. Of course."

A few minutes later, Bo came back down the stairs. "Nice

little place up there," he said. "Don't suppose you're looking to rent it out?"

"Why?" I asked. "You ready to leave me so soon?"

"I'm graduating in like four weeks, Mom."

"And going to community college." I crossed my arms. We'd been through this. Bo was getting a degree.

Bo sighed, but he gave me a quick kiss on the cheek as he left. "See you later, guys. Sink looks good, sir."

"Thank you!" Cav called as Bo departed.

"I'm actually heading out as well," Fiona said.

"To where?" Cav asked.

"I have an appointment in the next town over to look at some antique credenzas that might make for a nice little sideboard over here." She pointed to an open spot on the wall. I didn't have the heart to tell her that the bar she was decorating was taking on the look of a palace tea room and wouldn't have any room for dancing. We definitely did not need a credenza, whatever that was. But she looked so pleased with herself.

"I'll be staying over in a boutique hotel down there called the Roadside Inn," she added and I suppressed a cringe. It wasn't a nice place, but it was safe enough. And it meant Cav and I would have the place to ourselves for a while to try out his new bed.

"You're sure you can handle that on your own, Fi?" Cav looked worried as he stepped close to her.

"I'll need to gain some independence sooner or later, your–er, Cav. Might as well begin now." Fiona lifted her chin and picked up an overnight bag. "I'll see you later," she said, stepping out the door and leaving the prince and I alone.

"Should we test the bed?" Cav asked, a devilish gleam in his eyes.

I was tempted. But I also needed to stop by the diner and ask about the scheduling changes. I knew Arlene and Buzz were generally in on Saturdays, and I didn't want to miss them.

"Later we definitely should," I said, pressing myself close against him and dropping a hand to give him a quick squeeze. "But we have a few errands to run today."

"We do?" He sounded comically disappointed.

"We do."

We left the bar and headed to the diner, a strange sense of dread pooling in my belly as I stepped through the front door into the fry-oil scented air that had been my home away from home as long as I could remember. Arlene and Buzz sat in the corner booth, the diner's books open before them just like every Saturday in the past decade.

"Excuse me a moment," I said to Cav, seating him on a stool where Franny immediately swooped in to fawn over him.

"Arlene? Buzz?" I approached the back table feeling strangely nervous. "Can I talk to you a minute?"

They exchanged an odd look that I couldn't decipher, and then pointed to the bench across from them. "Sure honey," Arlene said.

"Well, I just wondered if there was something I'd done," I said. "Some reason I've been getting fewer shifts lately?"

"No, darlin', it's not you," Buzz said, his eyes sympathetic and sweet as ever.

"So...?"

Arlene shut the accounts book on the table in front of her,

and I noticed a gleaming ring I'd never seen before on her right hand.

"That's beautiful," I said, but Arlene slapped her other hand over the ring and pretended there was nothing out of the ordinary going on. "Oookay," I said, suspicion beginning to root around in my gut. Now that I was thinking about it, Arlene also had a fancy new haircut and wore glasses with little shiny stones all down the ear pieces. New, certainly. Expensive? Maybe. Even Buzz looked a little more refined in a Hawaiian print that looked a bit more fitted than his usual enormous short-sleeved button downs.

"Did y'all come into some cash?" I knew it was gauche to ask, but there was something fishy going on, and it wasn't just the lingering scent of last night's dinner.

"Er. Um..." Buzz stammered, not meeting my eye.

"It's fine," I said, feeling bad for pressuring them. "It's just. Guys. Bo's about to graduate, and I was saving up to try to pay for some classes at the college when he gets out. Things have always been good with us, but they're getting a teeny bit tight with my reduced shifts, and–"

"We didn't want to," Arlene said suddenly, practically on a sob.

"What?" I reeled back a bit. "Didn't want to what?"

Buzz put an arm around Arlene and then leaned in closer. "You know things have always been a little tight for us too, sugarplum," he said, and I sensed there was a big but coming. "But then we got a phone call. Mysterious-like."

"Someone with a very fancy accent promised to wire us a substantial amount of money if we let you go." Arlene practically cried the words and then threw her head onto her arms on the table, her ring catching the light.

Damn, that was a big stone.

"You haven't let me go, though," I pointed out, my mind still not quite in rhythm with my mouth.

"Not yet," Buzz said.

Fear churned through me. "You're about to?"

"Well..." Arlene lifted her head. "We don't want to. But it's a lot of money, and they were very specific. And so polite, too."

This had Prince Cav's family written all over it. Had they plotted some convoluted way to get him to come back by ruining my life? Did they even know about me? For a moment I considered whether Fiona could actually be working for the wrong side still, but then I remembered that she'd been wearing actual sneakers this morning. She'd definitely defected.

"I'm so sorry," Buzz said. "We were weak, and desperate..."

I shook my head, a strange lightness taking over where the fear and worry had been. Hadn't I been wishing for a reason to really invest myself in the business with Cyrus for a while anyway? Hadn't I been essentially acting as a general contractor for years, just without the pay or credit? "You know, I think it's okay," I told them.

"It is?" Arlene asked.

"It is," I confirmed.

I stood up, feeling freer, lighter than I had in years. And I walked to the place where my handsome boyfriend sat on a stool sipping a milkshake. "All set," I told him.

He looked up at me, his eyes darkening as he caught a whiff of the thoughts flitting through my mind. "Home?" he asked quietly.

"Home," I confirmed. "We have a bed to test out."

Cav sucked down the rest of his milkshake in one long slurp, tossed some bills on the counter, and practically carried me out to the car. Then he crumpled in the front seat, holding his head. "Ohhh, ohhh no," he moaned.

"Brain freeze," I said. "It'll pass."

When Cav had recovered, we drove back to the bar.

"What happened at the diner?" he asked as he pulled the key from his pocket and pushed open the door.

"Better question," I said. "What happened in here?"

Every available surface was covered with lacy paper doilies in every imaginable size.

"Fancy," Cav noted as he looked around.

"This smacks of Edith," I told him. "I was in her place once, and she has these things everywhere."

"Another joke?"

I shrugged. It wasn't terribly creative, but I supposed it qualified. "We need to plot our revenge."

Cav stepped close, putting his arms around my waist and caging me against the long wooden bar. "Later," he said, dropping his mouth to my neck. His tongue and lips began working their way along my throat toward my ear, and my breath began coming faster as everything else in me sprang to life.

"Later," I agreed, gasping when Cav's hands crept beneath the hem of my skirt and pulled it up so he could cup the globes of my ass.

Cav's head had lowered, pushing the V-neck of my tee down over one breast and then moving his mouth to suck and nip at the lace covering the other.

"Ohhh," I breathed as one of his hands slipped to the front

of my panties, pressing firmly and making a slow circle against the nerves there. "Oh."

"We will christen the bed later," he whispered. "But first, the bar." With that he hoisted me up, and then, to my shock, kicked off his cargo shorts and climbed to straddle me right there on the brand new, doily-covered bartop.

"I'll never order a drink here without thinking of this," I told him.

"Maxie, you drink free at Prince Cav's." He leaned down and took my mouth then, and we didn't continue the conversation. Instead, Cav slowly divested me of my clothing, bit by bit, and then surprised me by pulling a condom from his wallet.

"So prepared."

"I'm learning," he said, sheathing himself slowly.

"I've got something to teach you," I told him. And I pressed his shoulders back with my hands until he was lying on his back on the solid bartop, the bright sunlight slanting in from the high windows all around the sides of the space.

As he stared up at me with lust-filled dark blue eyes, I climbed over him, taking him into me inch by inch, until his pretty eyes rolled back in his head.

"Holy..."

"You're gonna want to watch," I told him, beginning to undulate on top of him, placing my hands on my breasts as I moved and tipped my head back.

"Fuck," Cav said, and I nearly stopped for the shock of hearing him curse. But it was all too good, too hot, too everything to pause.

I rode the prince—my prince—for all I was worth, feeling him fill every spare inch of me, from my heart to my toes, and the critically sensitive spots in between, which were beginning to tighten and twitch as I neared release.

"Maxie," Cav breathed, and I reached behind me, letting my fingers tease his royal balls. That sent him straight over the edge, and as I watched him let go, my own release came rushing after.

When it had subsided, I let myself fall over his warm chest, both of us breathing hard as we lay together on the bar top.

"What happened at the diner?" Cav asked again.

"They fired me," I told him, feeling freer still as I said the words. "Your family paid them to do it."

"What?" Cav sat up, holding me to him as indignation flamed in his eyes.

"It's fine," I said. "I think it was a change I needed but was too afraid to make."

"They're trying to get to me. They cut off my money, and maybe they think if they cut off yours too–"

"Let's not give them the satisfaction of thinking too much about it," I said. "I have a plan."

"You do?" Cav looked slightly relieved and he loosened his grip on my back.

"Yes, but first, the plan is to go up and try out the new bed."

"Right behind you."

We gathered our clothes and headed upstairs, trying out every piece of doily-strewn furniture we could find for the rest of the night.

Chapter Twenty-One
CAVANAUGH

Long after Max fell asleep I lay entwined with her and stared up at the ceiling, awake and angry. I'd tried a million times over the years to tell my parents that the royal life was not for me. I'd formally asked to be relieved of the duties thrust upon the spare. I'd been denied. I'd raged, I'd been ignored. I'd dug my heels in, I'd been slapped with more duties as a punishment for being difficult. Leaving in the middle of the night for America had been my last ditch effort to live my life the way I wanted to. Our people had the freedom to choose their profession and every detail of their lives, and yet I did not.

To add insult to injury, my brother was all too happy to be king one day. My parents truly did not need me and yet they'd been willing to ruin my life to have me wait in the wings "just in case."

Now, even in America, they'd found a way to try to strongarm me into doing what they wanted. They went after Maxine. When the sun came up, they were going to find that they'd crossed a line. I would not have Max's life ruined because they could not understand the word no. Sure, she seemed fine about pursuing other occupations, but that didn't negate the fact that they'd interfered and caused her harm.

I slid out of bed hours later, determined to put on a simple pot of coffee before facing my parents head on. I'd have to call, perhaps even fly back home to put a stop to their interference once and for all. I'd just gotten the water boiling when the front door of the bar opened. Fiona crept in, nearly jumping out of her new white tennis shoes when she saw me up. I wished I'd put a shirt on first, but perhaps she wouldn't notice I only wore boxers.

"Everything okay?" I asked quietly.

Her hair hadn't been brushed and there was a shirt sticking out of her half-zipped suitcase. Her eyes were frantic, which had me moving to her side. She was no longer my betrothed, but I wouldn't stand for her being harmed.

"There were *bugs*, Cav." She leaned in, eyes wide. "In the bed."

I winced. I wondered about that hotel. "You can stay here, Fi. We can get a couch or something down here."

Her eyes filled with tears, but some of the terror drained out of her. "I'm so sorry. I don't mean to interfere with you and Max, but I can't sleep with bugs! I'll just be here for one more night."

I smoothed a hand down her arm and tugged her over to the bar where I poured her a cup of coffee. "You're welcome to stay as long as you need. No one should sleep with bugs. Did I ever tell you about my first night sleeping in the back of the truck?"

Max came down the stairs in only my oversized T-shirt, the one with our family crest stamped on the breast, and slid into my side as I wrapped my arm around her. "Fiona is going to stay here tonight."

"Okay." Max squeezed Fiona's hand as it lay on the bartop, and I loved her for it. She didn't balk at my ex-fiancee staying in the bar. "Maybe we can join forces and convince Cav to spring for a fancy espresso machine so we don't have to drink instant coffee every morning."

Fiona brightened. "Oh! I bought one already!" She hopped off the tufted barstool and headed for a huge box in the corner of the bar.

"That's a coffee maker? It's the size of my truck." I had a feeling it cost quite a bit too.

"Oh hush and help us lift this baby," Max said with a smile.

I came over and on the count of three, all of us lifted the box and started to carry it over to the bar top. We were almost there when I kicked the electric drill that was laying out carelessly. Sadly, I thought I might have been the one to leave it out.

I howled and bobbled the box. Pain radiated up my toe and into my foot. The girls yelped at the shift in weight and somehow we got the thing down to the floor in one piece but Fiona was already on the floor on her knees.

"No dents, no dents" she whispered to herself, checking each corner to make sure her precious coffee maker was no worse for wear.

"You okay?" Max put her arm around me and I was all too happy to have her shoulders to lean on. My foot felt like it had a pulse.

"I think so. Can you break a toe by kicking a drill?"

"Oh dear!" Fiona finally looked up from the box and noticed my bright red foot. She leaned in closer.

The front door burst open again and all three heads turned to see who was here.

"Mother? Father?"

My parents were standing on the front doorstep, looking quite displeased with everything. In other words, they looked normal. Mother's nose lifted in the air. That is, until she took in the sight of Fiona on her knees in front of me, me in nothing but boxers, and Maxine's hands steadying me.

"What is this, Cavanaugh?" Father thundered.

I frowned, only then realizing what it must look like. I untangled from Max, sidestepped Fiona, and came forward, only limping marginally. Sympathy was in short supply with my parents so I knew complaining of a possible broken toe wasn't something to bring up.

"I'm glad you're here. We need to talk."

"I should say so! Is this why you left? So you could slum it up here in America with these two–"

"Careful," I growled.

Mother snapped her mouth shut, eyes burning. "We shall speak privately."

"Yes we shall. After I get dressed." I turned. "Let me introduce Maxine Waddell, though I bet you already know who she is." I lifted an eyebrow and mother's gaze skittered away. "Fiona, of course, you already know. They've been helping me immensely since I've been here so I expect you'll want to express your gratitude for their good care of your son."

Father made a noise in the back of his throat, but he didn't argue.

"Lovely to meet you, your majesties." Max did some weird

dipping thing with her knees that wasn't quite a curtsey or a bow.

"I'll be right back." I looked at Max and she gave me a slight head nod, indicating that she was just fine. I should have expected that. Maxine Waddell could handle anything life threw at her. I bounded up the stairs, getting dressed quicker than I ever had before. I didn't want to give my mother a second longer than necessary down there.

I heard the front door open yet again as I slipped a shirt over my head. I rolled my eyes. This place had turned into a train station with all the comings and goings. Wedging my feet into tennis shoes, I headed back downstairs to find an awkward standoff happening.

"Uncle Leo?"

His hand was still on the doorknob, as if he wasn't too sure he wanted to come in after all. He flicked a glance at me. "Came to tell you to prepare for a visit, but looks like I'm too late."

Father stood up tall. "Guess your sources are a little sloppy."

Uncle Leo crossed his arms across his chest. "Is that really what you want to talk about with the brother you haven't seen in a decade?"

Father's face turned an unhealthy color of red. I stepped forward to intervene, pulling Maxine with me. Fiona slinked to the back of the bar and I didn't blame her for wanting to escape this messy situation.

"I have a lot of work to do today, so I'd prefer you table that heartwarming reunion 'til later." My parents turned to me, irritation clear on their faces. "I am not returning to Mardelvia so you might as well turn right back around and go home. The kingdom is in good hands with Archie."

Mother stepped forward, her nose finally dropping and tears welling up in her eyes. "But Cav, you mustn't. The country needs to see a united front from our family." She side-eyed Uncle Leo. "We can only have one defection per millennia or the people's confidence in us gets shaken."

I tightened my grip on Max's hand. "I understand where you're coming from, but I will not put others' perceived emotions ahead of my own happiness, Mother. I can return for special occasions but I will not be living there. I've already built a life here. In Sailfish Banks. And with Max."

Mother came closer to stand in front of me, studying my face for long moments. Then her gaze flickered over to Max before returning to me. "You are in love, son?" she asked quietly.

"Very much so. I intend to marry Maxine as soon as I have this business up and running."

Father pushed my mother aside gently, but the anger on his face was anything but gentle. "We did not raise you to just leave the country when you feel like it. Give me back the ring. Now."

"Archie," Mother whispered, hand landing on his chest.

"No, Caroline." Father's familiar stoic expression hardened as he glowered at me. "If he wants to defect, then we will cut him off as he wishes. Maybe then he'll see the folly in his grand plan."

I nodded, my heart sagging in my chest. All this time, I'd hoped they'd come to see my side. I'd hoped they would give me their blessing. Instead, my father wanted to cut me out of his life like a tumor. So be it.

"Let me go upstairs and get it."

Chapter Twenty-Two
MAXINE

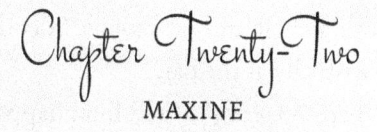

Cav disappeared up the stairs, and I did my very best to appear calm, put-together, and refined. As much as that was possible in a big white T-shirt, panties, and a case of bed head caused by a long night rolling around with the royal son of the very grumpy couple before me.

Cav's mother–the queen, I realized–was looking at me in a way that made me think she was trying very hard to see exactly what it might be that Cav had fallen for. But it didn't bother me too much in light of the fact that Cav had just announced he planned to marry me. My feelings were turning somersaults inside of me, and I was tempted to do a little shimmy, but I knew enough to be sure that would be the wrong move altogether in this particular scenario.

"So," I said, deciding to go for casual. "Can I offer you a seat? A cup of coffee?"

Cav's father turned to look at me as if he was just realizing I was still in the room. His look was definitely what I'd construe as withering, and I began to sweat under the weight of his silent disapproval.

Leo pulled out a chair and sat heavily. "I could use a beer," he said, looking wistfully at the bar.

"Not quite there yet, Leo," I told him, happy to receive the quick grin he shot my way.

"Erm, your, uh. Your majesties." Fiona was suddenly at my side, having pulled herself back together behind the bar. "May I present Maxine Waddell officially? Things were a bit, erm... awkward when you came in."

"They certainly were," Cav's mother said, and I thought she almost smiled as she looked at me again. "Fiona," she went on, taking a seat at one of the antique tables, "I must say, I really see no reason for you to continue with this ridiculous little escapade. Your mother is beside herself. Pleasure to meet you, Maxine."

Fiona looked nervously at Cav's father, who continued to loom near the door like a malicious statue.

"Oh, Archie, do sit down," Cav's mother finally said. When he did, lowering himself resentfully into a tufted chair, she waved for Fiona and me to do the same.

"I don't have any plans to return, your majesty. I very much regret having failed you both–"

"Spectacularly," Cav's father interjected.

"Erm. Yes, well. That said, I believe I will stay here to seek my own path, as Cav has done."

"Cavanaugh has merely sought a way to further embarrass our family and sully the royal crown. And where IS that ring?" He shouted this last part angrily, leaning toward the bottom of the stairs.

"Oh, for fuck's sake, Arch," Leo moaned. "Not everyone wants to be royalty!"

"Of course they do," Cav's father said. He glanced at me. "And most will go to any lengths for it."

He thought I was hoping to become royalty? That was funny, since I hadn't even known Cav was part of a royal family when I fell for him.

It had taken Cav a bit longer than I would have thought necessary for him to find the ring at this point. He'd had it just a couple days ago, it couldn't have gone far.

"I'll just go see," I said, figuring I could grab my shorts and tank top while I was up there.

I darted up the stairs and stopped short to see Cav sitting on the bed, staring at the floor between his feet.

"Cav?"

He turned to look at me, his face stony and something in his gaze that made my heart drop into my stomach. "The ring is gone."

I stared back at him for a second, and then stepped closer, pulling my clothes from the chair by the bed and stepping into my shorts. "What do you mean? You just had it."

He nodded, his gaze still cold as he watched me put my bra and tank top on. "I did. And I showed it to you. And to Bo."

"Right. And then where did you put it?"

He pointed to the top dresser drawer, which was pulled open and had clearly been searched, socks hanging out of it on both sides.

"Are you sure? Maybe it was one of these other drawers," I said, turning and reaching to open one of the adjacent drawers.

"I searched them all. It's gone."

I couldn't help it. I repeated his search, but I came up empty too. I turned back around to face him. The cold look in his eyes sent another cold sliver of worry through me.

"Bo was up here yesterday."

The worry coiled in the bottom of my stomach and bubbled there, frothing into something that was perilously close to anger. "To fix the sink," I said, my voice even as I realized what he implied.

"He's the only one who could have taken it," he said.

"My son did not steal your family ring," I said, straightening my spine and feeling every mama-bear defense I had preparing for a fight. Even as I said the words, though, a teeny-tiny question arose in my mind.

Could Bo have done this? Or could one of his friends?

"Unless you have it, Maxine, there is no other answer."

"Fiona?" I suggested, realizing immediately how impossible that was.

"We need to talk to Bo."

"Cav," I said, taking his hand and using the tone of my voice to pull his gaze to mine, hoping he'd talk about this reasonably.

But Cav pulled his hand from mine and shook his head. He'd already decided what had happened. He'd already judged Bo, and me, in the process.

"Son? This is taking far too long." Cav's father's voice boomed through the space around us, and Cav rose, shaking his head.

"You have no idea what he's done in taking that ring," Cav said to me. For a second, a flicker of warmth in his eyes reassured me, but then it shuttered again, and Cav's handsome jaw set as he turned to descend the stairs.

I followed him down, trying to decide which emotion to handle first: anger that he'd accuse my son so quickly of something terrible, or hurt that he suddenly didn't seem to feel anything for me at all.

"How dare you accuse my son, and me!" I hissed at his back. "How dare you assume that just because we don't come from money and palaces and fancy family rings, that we'd jump at the chance to steal yours!"

Cav turned back around as he reached the bottom of the stairs. "Max–"

"No." I stomped past him and into the space below. "I'm going home. Good luck figuring out all of"--I waved my hand to indicate everyone in the room and the entire situation–"this."

"Max?" Fiona said, her voice full of worry.

"Nice meeting you all," I told the group, and then stormed out, slamming the door behind me.

Chapter Twenty-Three
CAVANAUGH

Max stormed out, clearly angry at me for even suspecting Bo. Fiona looked at me like I was an idiot in need of a time-out. My father appeared ready to punch me in the face and Mother wasn't much better with her teary-eyed stare. To top it all off, my ring was gone.

A family member hadn't lost one of the exclusive rings since 1892 when robbers held the reigning prince at gunpoint outside a brothel and took it off his finger. He'd gotten it back the next day, of course, along with the heads of the two robbers. Simply losing it in my attempt at running away from the crown was not what I wanted to go down for in our country's history books. In fact, I wasn't even sure what the punishment was for losing the ring, but I could only imagine it wouldn't be good.

"What is it now?" Mother asked, blinking back tears that were at odds with her glare.

I squared my shoulders and faced the shit head on. "I need to go speak with someone first. Why don't you check into a hotel and we can meet tomorrow morning?"

"Not the Roadside Inn," Fiona whispered helpfully.

"We have a room at the Four Seasons in Sunset Point," Father sniffed.

"Oh sure, ruin my town," Uncle Leo grumbled.

Father turned sharply, giving Uncle Leo a glance that would have incinerated most men. Uncle Leo, having grown up with Father, didn't seem to mind one bit. As much as I could have stayed longer and watched these two grown men spar like children just for the entertainment value, I had something more important to do. I had to find Bo.

The old truck barely turned over as I cranked the engine. It rumbled over the dirt lot slowly, letting out a backfire right as my mother opened the door to step out of the bar. She toppled backwards into Father, but I was busy trying to miss the fleet of black sedans that idled at the curb, our country's flag waving from the front antenna of each one.

Sailfish Banks flew by my window as I drove out to Max and Bo's place. Absolutely none of it looked charming and inviting right now. Dark clouds hovered over the ocean, a sure promise of an afternoon thunderstorm. Those clouds were as dark as my thoughts.

Perhaps naively, I'd felt like Max and Bo and I would be a family soon. I thought that, given enough time, Bo would accept me into their small circle. All the while, the unruly teen was planning to rob me.

I almost didn't see him as I made my left by the gas station. It was the country music pouring out of the silver sedan that caught my attention. My head swiveled and I hit the brakes when I saw Bo's handsome face looking obstinate. A shorter guy in a polo and expensive sneakers, standing in front of a giant truck with all the bells and whistles had his arms crossed over his chest. There was a fight about to happen and I was just the right level of angry to get involved.

I parked the old truck half on the curb, half on the street and walked over to the group of guys squaring off. I recognized Gator and Colby, but the shorter guy must have been the elusive Tony Russo, judging by the apparent wealth he displayed.

"You've had weeks. I want my money."

Gator shifted on his feet, his hands clenched into fists by his side. "I got something, but I need a few days to sell it. You'll have your precious cash, Russo, don't worry."

"My dad's on me, man. That paint job is your fault."

"Dude, he knows," Bo interjected. "He said he needs a few days, but he'll have it."

Russo wrinkled his nose and then chewed on nothing, trying to look like a tough guy when he could probably barely see over the steering wheel of that truck of his. "You better."

"What do you have, Gator?" I asked, joining the group. All heads swiveled in my direction.

"Who the fuck are you?" Russo spat.

I turned my gaze on him and he shrunk back. I'd learned from dear old Dad how to speak with my facial expressions. "I suggest you leave now."

Russo studied me. Meanwhile I didn't blink. He finally dropped his hands and stepped back. "Fine. Whatever. Just have my money, Gator." He nodded at his buddies and they all climbed into his truck. He revved the engine on his way out but I'd already turned back to Gator, Bo, and Colby.

"I understand you three have something of mine. I suggest

you return it before I get the authorities involved." I had no intention of doing that, but getting my parents involved would be worse.

Bo pushed in front of his friends. "Cav? What are you talking about?"

I held my hand out and kept my focus on Gator. The second Tony Russo pressured him about the money to fix his dad's boat, it all made sense. Gator was in a money crunch and had seen an opportunity. It only made me slightly feel better that Bo hadn't taken it, but he must have been in on it. He and Max were the only two people who even knew about the ring.

"It's time to return the ring."

"We didn't take no ring," Colby drawled, clearly not understanding the importance of said ring.

Gator shuffled his feet and wouldn't meet my gaze. I towered over him, thankful that he was only seventeen and hadn't put on much bulk yet. "So if I searched your pockets right now, I wouldn't find it?"

Gator's head lifted and he jerked back. "You can't search my pockets!"

I shrugged and pulled my phone out of my jeans pocket to dial Emilio. "I'll call the police then and see if they'll search them."

Gator sputtered and turned to his buddies for help. I held the phone to my ear and waited for the phone call to connect with my best friend. Bo stepped forward and snatched the phone from me, hitting the end call button.

"Fine. I took the ring, but this has nothing to do with Gator."

I frowned, not wanting to believe that story at all. "You sure about that?"

Bo stuck his bottom lip out. "Yeah, I'm sure. I already sold it too. Sorry, old man."

Panic and deep disappointment waged for space in my chest. There wasn't much I could do, short of tackling each boy and searching their pockets for my property. I only had one card left to play and because of the steep price I'd pay for losing that ring, I was willing to play it.

I looked Bo right in the eyes, wondering why such a smart, handsome boy would choose to align with these troublemakers. "Your mother is going to be so disappointed in you."

His eyes shuttered and his shoulders sagged. Then I turned and walked back to my truck, angry, hurt, disappointed, and heartbroken at what this meant for Max and me. I had all day to figure it out while I visited every pawn shop in a fifty mile radius, trying to find that ring.

When my headlights bounced over the bar and apartment upstairs when I came home empty handed later that night, I didn't feel like Mardelvia was home any longer. But staying here in Sailfish Banks might not be the right answer either. Not without Max.

I was a prince with no country. A man in love with no partner.

Chapter Twenty-Four
MAXINE

Bo wasn't at home when I got there. Which was probably just as well, because I didn't like him to see me cry, and the mascara trails that had appeared in the short drive home were no joke.

Besides that, I wasn't sure how to approach him about this.

Trust was a delicate balance between a mother and her child. You go into the whole arrangement knowing that children–because they are human–are inherently untrustworthy. Throughout their childhoods, you look for every opportunity to teach them how to be kind, genuine, and careful, how to earn another human being's trust and keep it. And in the process, you show your child that he can trust you. Always. Completely.

Bo knew I always had his back. Because from the beginning it had been me and him. We'd always had only each other, and I'd done so many things wrong I couldn't keep track. But I'd never, ever broken his trust.

And now?

Now I had to ask him whether he'd taken that ring from Cav. If he had, and he admitted it to me... then I wasn't sure I'd ever trust him again, and it would signal my single biggest failure as a mother. And if he hadn't taken it but I ask him, essentially suggesting he had?

He'd never trust me again.

And then there was Cav... He'd looked at me with those cold eyes, and everything I'd believed lay between us had shattered in that moment.

He was a man who said he wanted something new, who told me he was seeking a new life, but who reversed directions completely as soon as that silly symbol of his royal heritage disappeared.

I mean, sure it was fancy. But for god's sake, it was only a ring.

I blew out a long breath, lifting my head from the steering wheel where I'd been leaning against my arms and sobbing pitifully in my driveway. Flipping down the visor mirror, I swiped at the makeup smeared beneath my eyes. As I pushed the visor back up and pulled the keys from the ignition, I reached for the door handle and let out a scream.

There was someone standing just outside the driver's door, staring in at me.

And it wasn't someone I'd been hoping to see.

"Brody? What the hell?" I pushed the door open and stood before Bo's father, staring up into the dark eyes I'd once thought were the most beautiful things in the whole world.

"Hey Max." Brody still had his rich-boy drawl, and at this moment, it sent every tiny hair on my body standing on end.

There had been times–years, really–when I'd wished for this

exact scenario. To come home and find Brody Hawkins here to tell me he'd changed his mind. To ask if I still loved him, if he could be part of Bo's life. Hell, maybe I'd been hoping for that right up until a few weeks ago when a certain wayward prince came into my life.

But I didn't wish for it now.

"What are you doing here, Brody? This is really not an ideal time." I closed the car door and crossed my arms, glancing around to make sure Bo wasn't going to pop up and create an even more complicated situation than we already had.

"I was in town seeing my folks," Brody said, giving me a lazy smile that had once melted the panties right off me. "Wanted to come say hi. See if I could take you and my son to dinner maybe."

I felt my jaw drop open, and I snapped it shut, squinting up at the man before me.

"Your timing is complete shit, you know that?"

"C'mon Max–"

"No."

"No?"

"No, you can't take us to dinner. No, you can't see your son. And no, you can't just appear here as if this is something that we do all the time. Do you know how old Bo is now? How many years it's been since you showed any interest in him at all?"

"Yeah, I know." Brody lifted a hand, rubbed it through his wavy blond hair. He still looked like some kind of surfer god, and if I didn't know better, I'd even think he was handsome. But maybe that was because he looked so much like my son.

"I'm sorry about that. It's just—I've been thinking about a few things. Could I come in? Could we talk?"

That was a bad idea. "I have a lot going on right now," I told him, starting for the front door.

"We can be quick," Brody said.

"Fine. Ten minutes. But Bo's not here." I pulled open the door to the cottage and Brody followed me in. I was struck again by how ironic it all was, Brody Hawkins finally showing up at my door on the day my heart was shattered by another man choosing something else over me. I'd told myself all these years that Brody's choice was about him, that I was a good person, a catch, even. But now Cav had made it clear that his royal roots and a gaudy ring were more important to him than I was. So maybe the problem was me.

"Sit," I told Brody, pointing at the couch. I did not need him wandering around.

He did as I told him and I swept through the house, ripping Post-It notes off every visible surface.

Stupid affirmations.

Before I had to go sit with Brody and hear whatever it was he had to say, I grabbed my black marker and a yellow notepad and scribbled

You Come in Alone, and You Go Out Alone,

and stuck it to the fridge. I gave it a nod, then wrote one more.

The only person you can trust is yourself.

Good reminders.

I pulled a beer out of the fridge and took it to the table, sitting down and staring across the room at the man I'd once been stupid enough to love. "Tell me what you need to tell me and then head on back to your fancy life, Brody. I've got things to handle."

He watched as I opened the beer and poured it down my throat, clearly stunned. But then he started talking.

"I haven't done a lot of things right, Max. Not for years."

"Duh."

"Maybe you could just let me get through this?"

I gave him the universal sarcastic hand wave for "proceed" and finished the beer.

"I should have been there for you. For my son."

Nice to hear, but made no difference now.

"You've done a good job with him. I've been watching him from a distance, you know. When I'm in town. And my parents tell me things."

The grandparents Bo never got to have. Screw them.

"We're all really impressed with how well you've raised him on your own."

"Is there a trophy coming with this little speech?" I asked. "Can we just get on with it?"

Brody looked uncomfortable now, and I felt like I'd scored a minor victory.

"No Max, look." Brody leaned forward, fixing me with a gaze that held so much sincerity I almost wanted to listen to him. "It's just... I'd like to know my son. And I know that's a lot to ask, so I thought maybe–I mean, my parents and I discussed it, and–maybe I could help with college? If he goes, I mean."

I frowned at him. Was he really saying these words? "Are you talking about money?"

"Well, yes." He cleared his throat, dropped my gaze. "I mean, I guess maybe things haven't been easy for you–"

"I'll stop you right there," I told him, fury mixing with all the disappointment that had festered inside me for the last eighteen years. "I don't want your money, Brody. Not now. If you'd stopped by about sixteen years ago and helped out buying milk that I literally had to put spare change together to buy, maybe. Or if you'd shown up around the time that Aunt Glenda died and I didn't have enough money to pay for a proper funeral or a coffin, I might have taken you up on it." I rose, needing to feel bigger because he'd made me feel so small for too long. "But now? Now we're doing just fine, thank you. I've had eighteen years to prove to myself and to my son and to everyone else in this god forsaken place that money isn't what matters. What matters is believing in the people you love, being there when they need you. That's what matters, and that's why you are just too damned late."

Brody stared at me with a stunned expression as I stood before him with my hands balled into fists, breathing hard.

"Hey Mom." Bo chose that moment to stroll through the front door, skidding to a dead stop when he spotted Brody sitting on the couch. "Dad?"

"Mr. Hawkins," I corrected him automatically.

"Mr. Hawkins," Bo said, and I hated the hope and reverence in his voice. For eighteen years, Bo had known who his father was, had asked me if I thought he might ever come back, be a part of our family. Only in the last six years or so had his questions changed tone, and I'd been certain that he understood that this was a man who didn't deserve his love or even his thoughts. But Brody was Bo's dad, and there was a link inside them I couldn't alter whether I liked it or not. And now, Bo stood looking at the man who didn't want him, and it just about broke my heart.

"Mr. Hawkins was just leaving, and you and I have some things to discuss." I could hear the exhaustion in my own voice. I wanted to crawl into bed, curl up, and cry. But that had never been an option for me. Not in the past, and not today.

Bo looked at me then, and I watched the curiosity on his face morph to concern. His brows lowered and he glanced at Brody again. "Mom, have you been crying?" He spotted the beer. "And drinking?" My son's face darkened and he seemed to get bigger as he turned back to Brody, who still sat looking stunned on my couch.

"I think it's time for you to go," Bo told him.

"Bo, I just came to–" Brody stood, reached a hand out like he was hoping Bo would shake it.

"To upset my mother?" Bo's voice was low, menacing.

"Bo, it's fine. He was leaving."

"I wanted to apologize," Brody said, and part of me admired his willingness to step closer to Bo, who had a couple inches even on him. "I wanted to tell you that I know I screwed everything up, and that I'll always regret missing out on knowing you. I can see that you are a good man. That your mother did a wonderful job, and I just wanted to see if–"

"Brody, not today," I said, finally finding my nerve again. "There's a lot going on, and I need to talk to Bo."

Bo was still absorbing the words he'd certainly been wishing to hear for most of his life.

"Maybe another day?" Brody asked.

"Another day," I said, nodding and ushering him to the door.

He reached into his pocket and pulled out a folded piece of paper. "I know it doesn't make up for anything." He handed it to me, and I held it, watching Brody Hawkins walk down my front steps and away from my house.

I stuffed the paper into my pocket and turned to Bo, steeling myself for the question I had to ask. He stood still, looking at the spot where his father had stood, and my heart quivered inside me. Bo was a hulking man now, but every time I looked at him, I still saw that little tow-headed toddler with the big blue eyes, looking at me like I was his whole world. Because I was.

"Bo, sit down," I said, taking my place at the table again.

Bo moved around the coffee table and sat down on the couch where his father had been moments before.

"I need to ask you a question."

"I think I need to tell you something first."

I asked my question at the exact same time that Bo blurted, "I told Cav I stole his royal ring."

And at his confession, everything inside me came to a skidding stop, the light in the room fading until all I saw was darkness. The world I'd believed in, the one where I'd done a good job raising a kid on my own, the one where a man who was so out of my league it was laughable actually loved me? That world didn't exist.

Chapter Twenty-Five
CAVANAUGH

Something wasn't sitting right with me.

Several somethings, one of which was this bloody situation with Bo. Something had been off about his eyes when he told me he took my ring and sold it.

The moon came streaming through the windows all night long as I lay there wide awake, highlighting all the work we'd done on this place. Me, Max, and Bo. The boy-turned-man I'd gotten to know shoulder to shoulder while we hauled drywall and cleaned paint buckets didn't match with the one who'd confessed to stealing. I was ashamed to admit that it was past midnight when it finally hit me.

Bo was covering for his best friend.

I sat up in bed, my brain finally able to think clearly after all the things that had happened today. I'd been so lost in heartache over Max and the disapproval on my parents' faces that I hadn't been able to put it together until now. Bo hadn't stolen that ring. He might have told his friends about it though, and when push came to shove, Gator saw an opportunity and took it.

What I wanted to know was why Bo felt the need to cover for his friend. He knew stealing something that valuable wouldn't just go away. There would be punishment and possibly legal action. Bo was not a dumb kid. He was actually very smart and highly attuned to what was right and wrong. If he lied to cover his friend, there was a reason, and I wanted to know what it was.

The second the sun began to lighten the sky, I climbed out of bed and got dressed, slipping downstairs quietly so as not to wake up Fiona who'd made a bed of sorts out of blankets in the corner of the bar. I winced, realizing I should have gotten her a couch or something, but I'd clearly lost track of everything going on yesterday. I shut the door and climbed into my truck.

> I don't want to take this to the police. Meet me at the docks in an hour.

I waited for several minutes before I saw the bubble pop up that told me Bo had seen my text.

> Don't really care about the police, not after I told Mom last night. But I'll meet you.

I didn't answer, just tucked the phone in my pocket and headed to the downtown area to buy a cup of coffee that wasn't instant. Max and Fiona had been right. We needed that fancy espresso maker. Max had been right about a lot of things. If Bo confirmed my suspicions, then I was going to owe Max one hell of an apology for not trusting her son.

The docks were busy on the end with small fishing boats heading out for the day. The other end was mostly quiet, the fancy yachts gently rocking in the water. I wondered who they all belonged to. Now that I didn't have access to a yacht, I saw the irony. All those nice boats and hardly anyone ever used them. Half the damn town would be ecstatic to take one out for a joy ride, but no. They sat here empty.

I sat on the one and only bench on the dock, sipping my coffee and wondering what to do about Max. I already missed her and it hadn't even been twenty-four hours. I'd been willing to leave my entire family, my country, my future for a place unseen, but I wasn't willing to give her up. I needed her like these boats needed this water. She held me up and gave me life and purpose. I'd never met another person who could make my heart feel light in my chest simply by smiling.

A tall man with blond hair and the kind of good looks that belonged on a magazine cover for luxury boats stepped off the closest yacht and eyed me with suspicion. Ah, how the tables had turned. Only a month ago, I would have been the man stepping off the royal yacht, and now I was the nearly homeless guy slumming it on the docks.

I lifted my coffee in greeting, hoping not to be chased off the dock by security for the second time. "Meeting a friend shortly."

The man nodded once and walked past me, looking familiar. I couldn't quite place him, and I turned it over and over in my head when I should have been thinking of a way to make things up to Max.

"Cav?"

I turned to see Bo standing a few feet away, his hands jammed in his jeans pockets. "Have a seat."

He came forward and sat, keeping a healthy distance between us. His gaze was fixed on the water and his jaw was tight. I had to hand it to him, the boy was definitely turning into a man with the way he handled situations with his shoulders back and head held high. Now to get him to do what was right instead of making himself a martyr.

"Look, I know you didn't take it, so why don't you cut the shit and talk to me, Bo?"

His head swiveled and a smile tugged on his lips. "That accent saying the word shit is kind of funny."

I grinned. "You thinking you can protect your friend is admirable, but if you want me to stop cussing with an accent, you need to tell me the truth."

He sighed and rested his forearms on his knees, his head bowed. "Gator can't pay that asshole."

"I presume you mean Tony Russo and the money Gator owes him for jacking up his dad's boat?"

Bo lifted his head and leaned toward me, suddenly full of energy. "Russo started that shit. It wasn't Gator's fault. Besides, Gator could never come up with that kind of money and Russo knows it."

While I could see he was anxious about his friend, I didn't think he understood the gravity of the situation. I'd talked with Fiona, who suggested I could be court martialed for losing the ring, never mind the familial repercussions. "I understand Gator is your friend, but stealing is never justified."

Bo lost some of the heat in his eyes. "I know. And I'm sorry. I had no idea Gator had it. They were teasing me about Mom dating the new guy and I may have said something about your family being loaded. I swear I didn't tell them about you being from a royal family though."

I nodded. "I believe you, but I need that ring back. Since you don't have it, I need you to get it back from Gator."

Bo flopped back against the bench. "See, the thing is, Gator's family sucks. His mom is an alcoholic and he has a little sister. She's only seven, Cav. If Gator doesn't pay back Russo, he'll have him arrested. If Gator's not there to protect his sister, his mom's latest boyfriend can't be trusted, if you know what I mean."

The gravity of the situation on Bo's end hit me full force. He and his friends were dealing with issues kids should never have to think about. "How about this? If you get that ring back for me, I can promise you that I'll pay back whatever he owes Russo's family? He won't be arrested and he'll be there to take care of his sister."

"You would do that?" Bo asked, hope lining his voice.

I clapped my hand on his shoulder. "I'll do it for you, son." I just wished there was something more I could do.

Bo swallowed hard and then gave me a firm nod. I stood and threw my coffee in the trash can by the bench. Now that this issue was solved, I felt a strong pull to get to Maxine. "Let's go talk to your mom. I bet she's feeling pretty miserable right about now."

Bo winced. "I think I made her cry."

My heart twisted in my chest. I had a feeling I had a lot to do with those tears too. I wasn't sure if she'd forgive me for not trusting her son and, ultimately, her parenting, but I had to try. My entire future depended on it.

"Come on. Let's go make things right."

Chapter Twenty-Six
MAXINE

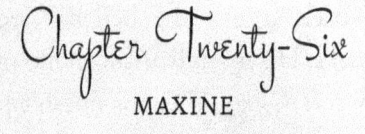

I woke up the next morning thinking I couldn't remember the last time I'd been so disappointed in Bo. Or in myself. What kind of mother raises a kid, so completely oblivious of his true nature? I'd spent eighteen years believing that I was doing the right things, bringing up a man who knew right from wrong, who wanted to live an authentic life, who was proud of who he was and where he'd come from.

But I guess Bo wanted more. More than I could give him. And he wanted it badly enough to steal for it. To steal from someone who'd been kind to us. Someone I loved.

I sat on the couch for a long time after Bo had slunk back out the door, looking almost as defeated as I felt. My instinct was to race after him, to apologize for yelling. To take back some of the disappointed words I'd hurled at him. But I knew that if he had any chance left of figuring out what was right, he had to see how his actions had hurt other people. He had to see that there were consequences to his choices.

My heart literally ached inside my chest.

It felt like in the course of one day I'd lost absolutely everything. And, god, it hurt.

I'd set a timer on my phone when Bo left. Thirty minutes. That was how long I'd give myself to fall apart. And at the end of thirty minutes, I was going to have to go on. I was going to have to move forward, no matter what I'd lost today.

That thirty minutes had been the worst of my life. I cried like I hadn't since the day my parents had sent me away. I sobbed every ache and disappointment and tiny bit of sadness out of me, and yet a bottomless well of despair remained, even when the timer went off.

"Nothing to do but take a step forward," I told myself, shutting off the overly peppy sound of my timer. "What choice do I have?"

I grabbed a sticky pad and scrawled a note.

The only choices are the ones you make for yourself.

I'd wiped mu nose on my sleeve and rubbed away whatever mascara might have been left below my eyes, and then I'd stood, gulping down the tears that continued to threaten and putting myself to bed.

The next morning as I rolled over, the previous evening rushing back, my phone rang just as I considered sinking back down and giving up altogether.

I sniffed and answered it. "Hello?"

"Max. It's Cyrus."

"Oh, hey Cyrus. I was gonna call you in a bit, actually."

"Yeah?"

"Yeah. Nevermind. What's up?" I didn't feel like getting into a whole negotiation right then, though I knew I'd need to figure out my next career steps soon and Cyrus would be a big part of that.

"Well, I have a proposition for you."

I wandered into the living room and sank down onto the couch. "Okay."

"You okay, Max? You don't sound like yourself."

I didn't feel like myself. I wondered if I ever would again. "Yeah."

"Well, here's the thing. I don't know if you'd ever consider it, but I need a GC. I've been getting a ton of new jobs, and it's just a lot to handle. You're already basically working as a general contractor anyway, and I just thought maybe you'd wanna do it full time. You're more connected than most of the guys calling themselves contractors around here anyway."

"I... uh..." That was exactly what I'd wanted to propose to Cyrus. "I think–"

My words died on my tongue because as I spoke, Cav and Bo appeared on the doorstep. Together.

"I have to go," I told Cyrus. "I'll call you later."

"Okay, Max, but don't leave me hanging too long. I'm kinda desperate here."

I didn't have the ability to answer him, and wasn't sure I actually hung up either, but a moment later, my phone was on the table in front of me and Cav and Bo were inside, both of them looking at me uncertainly.

Words were on the tip of my tongue, but that was exactly where they remained. I couldn't speak at all.

"Max," Cav said. His eyes were warm and deep again, he'd

lost the stony glare that had shattered my world the day before. But it didn't matter. It was too late, wasn't it?

The words arrived. Better late than never, right?

"No." I shook my head and stood. "Whatever this is, I don't think I want to do it right now. I've had more than enough of both of you today, and until I've had some time to think about everything, I just am not sure I should be around either one of you–"

"Mom." Bo's voice cracked, and I swung my gaze to him, working hard to see the man–the thief–and not the toddler who'd nestled in my arms like I was his whole world.

I ripped my eyes from his, staring at the note I'd written myself. "No," I heard myself whisper.

"Max," Cav said, pulling my head up once more. His voice was a soft plea, and it pulled at pieces of me that had been only his, pieces I'd given away so freely, not realizing how much it would hurt to have them broken. "Please, listen for a moment. I know you're upset, but I believe you've got it wrong."

Anger and hurt brought my eyebrows down low as I looked between the two men who'd hurt me. "I don't think I do."

"Mom, I didn't steal Cav's ring," Bo said, stepping forward and taking my hand, forcing me to look up at him again. "He made me tell him the truth, and he knows I didn't take it."

"Then who did?" I asked, too confused to feel any relief.

"Gator took it, Max," Cav said, putting a hand on my son's shoulder, as if to protect him. My heart vibrated within my chest at the fatherly gesture.

"Gator."

"He didn't have a choice," Bo said, but with a little squeeze from Bo, he added. "I mean, stealing is never the best choice.

But he felt like he didn't have a choice. He needed the money to give Russo so Russo didn't call the cops about his boat. If Gator got taken away, Lizzie wouldn't have anyone." His eyes shone and my heart threatened to give up its tough-heart act. "Mom, she's only seven. You know their mom's a mess."

"Bo was covering for his friend."

That was a lot to take in.

"Max, darling, can we sit?"

I looked around, opening my eyes wide and taking a deep breath as if I'd just swum up to the surface and broken through, my head finally above the murky depths. "Yeah. Let's sit down."

We did, one man on either side of me on the couch. Cav rested a hand lightly on my leg, and Bo took my hand.

"I'm sorry I lied, Mom. I didn't know what else to do."

I frowned at him. "You tell the truth, Bo. That's what you do." I leaned forward, snatching my hand from his and wrote him a sticky note, pasting it on his big chest.

The truth is always the right path.

Bo stared at me for a moment and then gently took the notes and the pen from my hand and wrote another note, which he stuck on the table in front of me.

Not if it gets your best friend sent to jail and his little sister sent to foster care.

I sighed. But then I remembered I was still angry at Cav. I turned to face him. "You!"

He leaned back slightly like he thought I might hit him.

"You were so ready to believe Bo had taken your precious ring. Or that I had! And you were so worried about it that you were ready to throw away everything."

There. I was mad again. I crossed my arms and blew out a little huff.

Cav reached for the sticky notes and Bo handed them over.

I would never throw away what we have.

You are all that matters to me.

The ring is silly, but if I don't get it back, I'll go to prison in Mardelvia.

The table was littered with sticky notes now.

"That's ridiculous," I told him. "It's a ring."

"It represents the sovereign monarchy of the country and is meant to symbolize the peoples' faith in our family. If it is lost, the faith is lost. And he who loses it will be blamed." Cav shook his head.

"I'm still mad that you thought we took it." It wasn't going to be easy to get past this. "I'm angry that you thought so little of me, of my son—"

"It wasn't that at all. I didn't even have time to think," he said. "My father was there, staring me down, and I knew I had to go back downstairs and show him yet again what a failure his second son was. That's how it's always been with us, you know."

"I didn't know."

"Hey, I might just..." Bo said, standing.

I swiveled to look up at him, giving him my best I'm-still-pretty-mad face.

"Gonna go see if I can find Gator. Maybe get it back."

I nodded.

"Sorry Mom."

Bo backed out the door and I turned back to Cav.

"Max," he said softly. "Please forgive me."

I wanted to be mad on principle. But I was also tired. Really, really tired of being angry and hurt. My insides had been in a hurricane all day and things were only beginning to clear up. But there was destruction left behind.

"It hurt to think you were letting everything go so easily," I whispered. "That you'd just throw it away over the things you told me you wanted to leave behind."

"I do want to leave them behind. And I could never let you go." He gazed into my eyes, and I saw the truth in his apology there, the love I'd felt between us. "Max, you raised a great kid. He was just trying to protect his friend."

"Yeah."

"Can we fix this?"

I dropped his gaze and picked up a sticky note, writing,

Forgiveness is the first step.

Cav's face scrunched up and he looked at me with a question in his eyes. "So do I have forgiveness?"

I nodded.

"What is the next step?" he asked.

I wrote:

That thing you do with your tongue.

He laughed, loudly and heartily, and my little house was full with the sound of it. "Okay, but we have to be quick. We really do need to get that ring back. Plus, I made a promise to Bo I need to keep." He stood and swept me off the couch into his arms, pulling me tight against his chest as I broke into a surprised giggle and my feet kicked in the air. "But first, my promise to you."

He moved quickly, carrying me into the bedroom where he made good on the promise he'd made.

Chapter Twenty-Seven
CAVANAUGH

Everything seemed surmountable with Max's hand in mine as we approached my building. The string of black sedans lined my property, which meant my parents were here, probably eager to grill me about the current situation and how I planned to fix things. Max tugged on my hand before our shadows fell on the front door.

"Could you really go to prison?" she whispered.

I pulled her into me, seeing the concern flooding her eyes. "It's a possibility, but I have faith things will work out."

Max shook her head. "I don't mean to be a pessimist, but Gator probably sold that ring the second it was in his hot little hands."

I leaned down and kissed her, wishing I had time to drag her into my bedroom and prove to her that all that mattered was her and me and this life we were building together. "In all the towns in all of the world that I could have run to, I came here and met you. I don't think I had much of an opinion about fate before, but I firmly believe in it now. I was destined to come here and fall in love with you, Maxine Waddell." I kissed her again, just because I could. "It will all work out."

She didn't look totally sold, but she let me lead us into what would soon be the best bar in all of Sailfish Banks. My parents sat at a table in the middle of the room like they were holding court at the palace. Father was on the phone and barking orders. Mother was wringing her hands, her head popping up the second we opened the door. She stood, her shoulders rolling back and her head held like she was balancing an invisible crown of jewels on it. Thankfully, they'd left the real crowns at home. Not that the fleet of sedans and personal security allowed them to blend in.

"Cavanaugh." Mom came forward and searched my face. "Did you find it?"

I shook my head and watched her face fall. I hated to disappoint her, more than my defecting had already, but I didn't want any further lies between us. The door burst open behind us and we all turned. Uncle Leo narrowed his eyes at my father before focusing on me.

"I asked around but no one has seen it."

My heart sank. I'd been to the pawn shops, Uncle Leo had asked his sources, and now it was best to accept that it was truly lost. I had little faith in Bo succeeding with Gator. Mother let out a pitiful yelp before jamming her hand to her mouth. Max leaned heavily into my side, as if wanting to soak me in before I was pulled away from her and tossed in a Mardelvia prison.

Father sighed and stood, his substantial bulk lumbering toward us. He'd put on more weight than Uncle Leo as he'd aged, but then again, he had quite a bit more stress running an entire country. A pang of guilt hit me for leaving, along with a sigh of relief that this would not be my fate.

"I have a plan. We'll have a jeweler make a fake."

"Archie!" Mother was shocked.

"Just until the ring can be tracked down. It'll buy us more time and keep Cavanaugh out of the dungeons." Father eyed me and it wasn't all disgust and disappointment in his blue-eyed gaze. There was an element of actual concern.

"I appreciate that." I stood as tall as I could, pulling Max under my arm. "I'm truly sorry that it's come to this. While I don't hold the ring in high regard due to the restriction it comes with, I do hold the symbolism in high regard. I'm grateful for my family, for the opportunity to work for the crown, and most importantly, for my country. But the ring signifies a life I will no longer allow for myself. I wish to stay here in North Carolina and make a life with Maxine. I wish to be absolved of my position and title."

Mother shook her head. "No, son. You will be absolved of your position, but not your title. The door is always open, as it should be in families. Your brother will make a fine king and all will be well."

The door opened again. Frankly, it was getting crowded. Bo, Gator, and Colby shuffled into the space. We stared at them and they stared at us. Well, not Gator. He was currently studying his dirty sneakers like they might hold the answers to the universe. Bo shoved him with his elbow and his head popped up. Gator lifted his arm expectantly. I frowned, putting my hand out. He opened his fist and my ring dropped into my palm. The entire group let out a sigh of relief.

"I'm sorry. I shouldn't have stolen it from you. Won't happen again." As far as apologies go, it wasn't half bad.

"I should hope not, considering you'll be in jail," my father rumbled, sounding every bit the king he was.

I could see Gator quaking in his shoes. "If I may," I interjected, reaching into my back pocket. "No one is calling the police on you, Gator. In fact, I have some cash that might help you out of your situation with Tony Russo."

I handed Gator all the cash I had left. It should have gone toward building the tiny homes on my property, but helping Gator and his little sister was more important. Gator's face turned red, but as he stared at the money his spine straightened, as if the weight of the world had been lifted. He lunged and pulled me into a back thumping hug before I could blink. Then he and his friends were turning to the door.

"Thanks, Cav. I'll make sure it all goes to Russo." Bo gave me a solid head nod before leaving with his friends.

"You gave the thief *cash*?" Father began to sputter, his face red.

I waved off his concern. "It's a long story, but his little sister was in trouble. That's why he needed money. Gator knows what he did was wrong. At least this way we can help his family while also honoring my family."

I slid the ring onto my finger one last time, looking down at my family crest and feeling a sense of pride about where I'd come from. There was also relief when I pulled it off again and handed it to Mother.

"I appreciate you letting me keep my title." I turned to Max. "As long as you're okay with dating a prince?"

Max beamed at me. "You'll always be my prince."

I hugged her to me, ignoring the tension in the room as Father and Uncle Leo glared at each other and Mother stifled her tears.

"May I speak with you alone for a moment, Cavanaugh?" Mother took a deep inhale and her tears began to dry.

I kissed Max's forehead and let her go to take Mother's elbow. We went upstairs and as she eyed my new apartment, she pulled a diamond ring off of her right hand. She held it out to me.

"This was my mother's wedding ring. I will give you my blessing if you promise to give it to Maxine when you propose. I want the Barclay legacy to continue, with or without you in the country."

I took the ring from her and pulled her into a hug. "Thank you, Mother. That's a ring I can accept. I'm not defecting from our family, I promise."

She squeezed me tighter. "Have the wedding in Mardelvia and you'll be my favorite."

I gasped. "Mother! Wait 'til Archie hears of this."

Her shoulders began to shake with laughter. "I shall simply tell him you lie. You're a defector and all. Completely untrustworthy."

I joined her in laughter, happy we could still be our old selves. Happy that she–and possibly my father, given more time–had accepted my plans. She finally let me go and stepped back, slipping back into the careful mask of the queen of Mardelvia.

"I must go downstairs and get to know my future daughter-in-law."

I dipped my head, trying and failing to hide my smile. "I plan to make that happen quickly."

Mother scoffed. "Just like your father."

I followed her down the stairs. "Don't say mean things, Mother."

Her tinkle of laughter made my heart lift. The mood downstairs was remarkably different. Max watched Father and Uncle Leo verbally spar like she was at a tennis match. I let it go on while Maxine and Mother got a chance to talk in the corner of the bar, but ultimately had to interrupt as diplomatically as I could when there was no end in sight. I pushed all three out the door as Max and I waved them off.

When every single sedan was off my property, I turned Max in my arms and wondered if now would be too soon to pop the question. The backfire of my truck startled us both. Fiona was back with some sort of curio cabinet strapped to the back of the truck. Max and I rolled our eyes at the same time and laughed. Fiona and her endless supply of furniture that was all wrong for the bar.

Now was not the right time to ask Max to marry me, but I promised myself it would be soon. In the meantime, I could tell her over and over how much I loved her. Before she turned to go inside, I pulled her back.

"I will always choose you and Bo, you can count on that."

Max's body melted into mine. "And I choose you, rich prince or penniless bar owner."

Chapter Twenty-Eight
MAXINE

For the next three weeks, my life was like some kind of daydream, only it was my real day to day that was blissful and candy colored. For a girl who'd spent the better part of her life scraping by, holding back a tidal wave with a teeny-tiny teaspoon to protect herself and her son, it was difficult to process. I had to pinch myself several times as Cav started spending more and more time at my house–eventually moving in with Bo and me. It was Bo's idea, actually.

"Mom, you're literally never home anymore because you're always over at that bar."

"That doesn't sound right," I told him, sitting at the small round table in our kitchen staring down at my laptop screen as I struggled to wrangle all the moving pieces of the latest development project Cyrus and I were working on.

"In any other family around here, it would mean something else, I guess," Bo laughed, taking the seat across from me. "But with your new job and your relationship with Cav, I hardly ever see you any more."

It was true, and guilt bubbled inside me. "I know, buddy. I'm sorry. I haven't been here as much as I should have been." I closed the laptop and looked over at my son, who was basically a full-grown man. One whose last moments of childhood I should have been hanging onto with both hands. "I'll stay over here from now on," I told him. "You need me."

"It's not that," Bo said, glancing down at the table and playing with the edge of the tablecloth. He looked up again. "Maybe Cav should just move in here?"

I tilted my head, trying to see if he meant it. A little thrill ran through me at the idea of waking up with Cav every morning, here in the house I loved so much.

"It would make sense. He could let Fiona have the apartment over the bar–"

"She's been pretty clear that even if it was available, ladies don't live in bars."

Bo smiled. Fiona was doing her best to fit in around Sailfish Banks, but she was never going to wipe off the veneer of etiquette and high society that clung to her like her pricey perfume. "Right. But still," he said. "It'd be nice to have this house feel full. It'd be like a real family."

"You know we are a real family, right? Even if it's just you and me?" It hurt my heart to think he'd ever thought anything else.

"That's not what I mean, Mom. You're the best mom there is and I've never wished for anything else. But maybe for a little while it'd be fun to live here with you and Cav together. The three of us." Bo looked more like his little-boy self in that moment than he had in years, and my heart pulsed at the knowledge that while I'd given him literally everything I could, a real nuclear family had been the one thing out of my reach.

I wondered if Cav would consider it.

That night, the three of us sat around that same little table, eating baked potatoes and steaks that Bo had cooked outside on the grill.

Cav's entire demeanor had relaxed since his parents had come through town, essentially blessing his decision to leave the crown and to embark on this new life. With us. He leaned back in his chair when we'd finished eating, his easy handsome smile making my whole body feel warm and light.

"Cav," Bo said, sipping at the beer in front of him on the table. "Can I ask you something?" He glanced at me. "If it's okay with Mom, I mean."

I nodded. I'd already told Bo how much I'd love it if Cav moved in, but I'd also told him I would ask him later. I guessed now was later.

"Mom and I were talking," my son went on. "And it seems silly for you both to be running back and forth every morning from your apartment or from here when all you really want is to be together."

A slow smile was spreading across Cav's face and his eyes sparkled.

"We wondered if you would consider just moving in here. With us."

Cav looked back and forth between Bo and me, and I could tell he was considering something before he spoke. Then he surprised me by standing up. "I have a different idea," he said. And then he moved around the table to stand between us, shot Bo a huge smile, and then dropped to a knee in front of me.

THE SPARE AND THE SINGLE MOM

I sucked in a gasp without meaning to. Was this really happening?

"Maxine Waddell," Cav said, locking his eyes to mine and taking my hand. "I arrived in Sailfish Banks, a man without a home, without a country–"

"Without a clue," Bo supplied.

I pushed down a nervous giggle and nodded at Cav encouragingly.

"And you were here. When I first met you, I knew my life was going to become something new, something I would never have recognized before."

"Didn't you guys meet in a Walmart dressing room? With Mom topless?" Bo asked, grinning.

"Bo, shush," I snapped. "Don't mess this up."

Bo raised both his hands and sealed his mouth.

Cav took a deep breath and looked up at me again. "I'm glad you're both here for this," he said, turning to Bo to pat his knee before turning back to me. "Because I know that when I tell you that you've changed my life and I don't want to consider what it would be like without you in it, I mean both of you.

"I love you. Both of you. And I'd like to propose that we marry, Maxine, and make this official." He glanced at Bo who gave him a thumbs up. "I proposed this idea to Bo a few days ago," he said, turning back to me, "And he's given me his blessing."

That sneaky kid. Joy welled up inside me and tears pricked at my eyes. I tried to focus on breathing.

"Max," Cav said, turning back to me and pulling a little box from his pocket. "Will you do me the extraordinary honor of agreeing to be my wife?" He opened the box to reveal a diamond ring that was honestly the most beautiful thing I'd ever seen. It was understated, not too big, not too small. The round diamond was flanked by two smaller stones, emeralds, I thought. And the band had an intricate pattern carved into it. It was gorgeous.

"Mom, answer." Bo prodded.

I found my voice just as my eyes found Cav's again, and the love and hope there stole my breath. "Yes," I managed, and I watched as if from above as Cav slid the ring onto my finger.

"This was my grandmother's ring, and my mother offered it to us with her blessing."

"Oh," I managed, words having abandoned me again.

Cav rose, tugging my hand, and I stood in front of him, looking up into the face I'd come to see in my dreams and all my best waking moments. "I love you, Max."

"I love you too, Prince Cav. Thank you for this. For everything."

"Mom, ask him." Bo's voice came from behind us.

"Oh. Right." I slipped my arms around Cav's waist, taking strength from the firm solidity of him. "Would you consider moving in here, Cav?"

He smiled down at me, the twinkle in his eye turning something over in my tummy. "I'd love that," he said. "I think Ben might be interested in the apartment, anyway."

"Ben?" I asked. That seemed strange. Ben had been around a lot, but I thought he had a whole life over in Sunset Point, where Leo's business was centered.

"He's considering a defection of his own," Cav said.

I nodded, not really caring who lived over the bar, as long as Cav lived here. "So that's a yes?"

"That's a yes. To life with the two of you. Come here, Bo." Cav reached one arm out, and my body felt warm and light as he pulled my son into our hug, the three of us sharing this incredible moment like we were meant to be together all along. Like a family.

Bo graduated from high school the following week, and he looked more handsome in his cap and gown than I ever could have imagined. Cav and Fiona and I sat in the audience, and across the aisle, I spotted Brody Hawkins wiping his eyes after Bo had walked across the stage.

When the ceremony ended and the crowd was on its feet, Brody found us just as Bo made his way to our little group.

"Hi Max," Brody said, and then he glanced at Cav. "Hello."

"Cav, this is Bo's father. Brody Hawkins."

"Hi Dad."

Cav greeted Brody, but the man's attention had already turned to his son, and I saw a look in his eyes of such obvious pride that it nearly broke my heart when I realized how much regret was mingled there in that gaze.

"I'm proud of you, Bo," Brody said. He turned to me. "And of you. You two are incredible. You've done so much–"

"With so little?" I asked, not wanting to ruin the day, but unable to help myself.

"No," Brody shook his head. "From what I can tell, you guys have everything. I've always hoped one day I'd find what you've got, but maybe it's just a little late for me." He glanced at Cav again, and then dropped his gaze. "I should get going and let you guys enjoy the day. I just wanted to be here for you, Bo, and tell you congratulations."

"Thanks," Bo said, and he shot a quick look at me, a question in his eyes.

I shrugged.

"Hey, Brody?" he said. "We're going to lunch at the diner. You wanna come?"

Brody's smile was wide and warm. "I'd like that. You sure it's okay?"

"The more, the merrier," Cav said.

We met Leo and Fiona at the diner, and Franny put us into the biggest booth in the far corner, giving me a hug before I sat down. I was so busy with my new gig as a general contractor, I hadn't had a lot of time to spend with my best friend, but part of me missed my previous life. It was simple and clear-cut. But this new life was better, even if I did have less time to catch my breath.

"To Bo," Leo said, holding his milkshake aloft as we all followed suit.

"To Bo," we all agreed.

"What will you do now?" Brody asked him.

"I'm signed up to start some college courses in the fall," Bo answered, surprising me. We'd talked about enrolling at the community college, but he hadn't mentioned it again. "I'm going to take a couple years, help get the tiny houses finished up with Mom and Cav, and then I think I'd like to learn about real estate development."

"Like me?" Leo said, sounding flattered.

Bo nodded. He and Leo had gotten to know each other in the last few weeks, but I hadn't realized what an influence the older man had had.

"Well," Leo said thoughtfully, "Ben doesn't seem to want to continue working for me, so there might be an opening soon."

"What's going on with Ben?" Cav asked. "Where is he, anyway?"

Fiona blew out an exasperated noise across the table, and everyone turned to look at her.

"Sorry," she said, raising a hand to her mouth. "It's just that this Ben person seems like quite a handful."

"Ben person?" I asked.

She looked between us then, her face a little guilty. "I've never met him, you know. You all talk about him constantly, but I'm not sure he really exists."

"Oh he does," Leo confirmed. "And he's a royal pain in my butt."

"Sounds right," Fiona said. "All I know of him is that every time I come back to the bar, things have been rearranged or something's been taken out or added, and it's always Ben's doing." Fiona didn't let emotion show easily, but she sounded very close to irritated.

"Well, you're bound to meet him soon," Cav said. "He's moving in over the bar next week once the first tiny house is completed for you."

Fiona frowned at that. "He is?"

"You'll like Ben," I assured her, though if I was honest, Ben was not my favorite person. He was nice enough, but he was a bit of a playboy. Nothing like his responsible cousin, Cav or his father, Leo.

"We'll see," Fiona said, but she did not sound convinced.

We finished lunch and there were a few minutes where we all milled around in the parking lot, saying our goodbyes. Brody pulled me to one side. "You never cashed the check, Max."

"Check?" I asked at the same time as the vague memory of him stuffing something into my hand weeks ago came back to me. "Oh, I forgot all about it. I think it's probably gone through the wash by now."

"It was for you. Should I write another one?"

I shook my head. "We don't need your money, Brody. But I think Bo would like it if you offered to take him to dinner now and then, or fishing. Maybe just get to know him a bit."

"He's a good kid," Brody said, gazing wistfully at his son, who was laughing with Cav as they said goodbye to Leo.

"He is. And he'd love to know you."

Brody nodded and gave me a kiss on the cheek just as Cav and Bo stepped near. Cav slid an arm around my waist and offered Brody a hand to shake. "Nice to see you again," he said.

"Thanks for coming," Bo said.

Brody glanced at the three of us. "Thank you for including me." He shoved his hands into his pockets. "I'm happy for you. For all of you. I hope maybe someday I'll find something like what you have."

"I hope you will," I told him.

"Maybe we can grab dinner soon?" he asked Bo.

Bo grinned. "Yeah. Definitely."

We watched Brody climb into his fancy car and head back to the other side of the island. I took a deep breath, loving the way the salt air filled my lungs as the summer sun beat down on us from above. The thick humidity hugged us close and I reveled in the embrace of the beautiful place I lived, and the certainty that everything in my life was exactly where it belonged. Bo on one side–every bit the man I'd raised him to be, and Cav on the other–every bit the man I'd hoped to find one day.

"I love you guys," I told them. "You both make me so happy I don't even know what to do with myself."

"I have ideas," Cav said, wiggling an eyebrow.

"And that's my cue," Bo said. He leaned down and gave me a kiss on the cheek. "I've got plans anyway."

"Don't get crazy," I warned.

"Mom, I'm taking Gator and his little sister for ice cream. I don't think it will get wild."

That was my boy. "Okay," I said, watching him walk away as Cav took my hand.

"He's a great young man," Cav said. "Because he has such a great mother."

I sighed and pressed myself against Cav's chest. "Let's go home, Prince Cav."

"Let's go home, Max."

Epilogue
CAVANAUGH

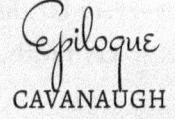

"I believe they want us to kiss," I whispered out the side of my mouth.

Maxine was a vision in white lace and tulle as she stood by my side on the high terrace. Somehow she loved me enough to put up with a wedding ceremony here in Mardelvia, led by my mother and her grandiose plans. We'd kept it small, only five hundred or so in attendance. I knew all of this would be a lot to deal with, so Max and I had snuck away to the justice of the peace in Sailfish Banks the day before we left and officially got married. Just the two of us. The way we wanted. But today was for my family. For my country. It was the least I could do after turning my back on my place in the palace.

Max winked at me. "I'm happy to oblige, Prince Cav."

I leaned down, a smile so permanently etched on my face these days I could barely give her the kind of kiss that would make the paparazzi happy. I hovered there, inhaling this moment, inhaling her. I never dreamed that life could be this good. This rich.

The crowd below cheered and the music and dancing began. Confetti rained down, landing on our heads. Thankfully, our attendance wasn't really necessary for the festivities to continue all night long. Mardelvia used every occasion as an excuse to celebrate.

"Come, you two. We have dinner with the court." Mother interrupted our moment, but all was forgiven when she took Max's hands in hers. "It's unspoken, but there's still pressure for a queen to have sons. I did my duty and have loved every second with them. However, I always wanted a daughter too. We may not be blood related, but by loving my son you are now my daughter and Bo is my grandson. Let there be no misunderstanding."

Maxine's eyes welled up, but she managed a regal head nod. "I appreciate that more than you know."

Mother lifted her nose in the air, her crown twinkling in the last rays of the sun before it set behind the hills. "I've also set up a trust fund for Bo, which I know you'll accept because I am his grandmother now."

With that announcement, Mother spun on her heel, hooked her hand on Father's elbow and the two walked back into the palace, a host of attendants scrambling after them. Emilio came over to pull me into a rough hug.

"I'm glad to see you this happy, friend."

I grinned. "All because you were willing to risk everything for me. I'll forever be in your debt."

Emilio rubbed his jaw. "I shall have to think of something expensive I want…"

I scoffed. "I'm penniless now. I can offer you a tiny house, but that is about it."

"I do not even know what a tiny house is, but I'll have to come visit."

"Please do."

We hugged one more time, thumping each other on the back before he went into the palace.

Bo waited until the balcony had cleared before coming up to us, looking older in the expensive suit Mother had given him for the wedding. He'd even trimmed his hair a bit for the occasion.

Max shook her head and kept blinking. "Is your mother for real?"

I smiled fondly. My parents were what Bo would call hardasses, but they had a strong heart inside their chests beating out an enduring love for their family and country. "As real as it gets."

Max shook her head back and forth, coming to grips with her new mother-in-law being a queen. "Think I can call her Mama?"

"You mean Granny Barclay?" Bo piped in, joining in on the joke.

I nearly choked. "I think she'd love it." She'd hate it. "How about we go eat so we can hurry up and get back home?"

"I'm in!" Bo nearly ran to get to the feast the royal kitchen had toiled over for days. The kid could eat more than four grown men combined.

Maxine stopped us when I put my arm around her waist and started to guide her inside. "Are you sure you're okay with Sailfish Banks being home? You truly don't mind giving all this up?"

Max had experienced the life of a royal for two whole days,

her jaw constantly dropped at the lavish surroundings, plethora of attendants for every little thing, and endless courses at each meal. We'd also had zero privacy.

I put my hands on her waist, holding her close and hoping she could see the truth in my eyes. "I will always love my country, but my home is with you, Max. Wherever we are together."

She studied me for a long moment. When her eyes went soft I knew she'd accepted my answer. "Sailfish Banks is a wonderful place to raise a child."

My heart lurched against my ribs and everything below the waist went tight at her meaning. "You want to have a baby with me, muscles?"

She twisted back and forth, just enough friction to drive me wild–and delay our entrance into the palace for a few minutes while I got myself under control. "I wouldn't mind a do-over, this time with the love of my life."

I leaned down and nipped at her lips, wishing we were home when she told me of her new interest. I was one hundred percent on board with the idea and figured immediately would be a good time to get started on that plan.

"I'm in, my love. All the way in."

The time difference, along with all the champagne that had been served at our wedding feast, was enough to have Max and I groaning as we arrived in Sailfish Banks. Gator picked Bo up at the airport to escape to whatever mischief newly graduated teens got into, while Ben picked up Max and me. He got us up to speed on everything he'd been doing to the tiny houses while we'd been gone. The first house was officially done.

"Could have had the second one done too if that woman hadn't delayed literally everything." Ben looked ready to throw punches.

"That woman?" I drawled, knowing full well who he meant.

Those two had been going at it since the day they met. I'd had to play referee more than once so no blood was drawn. For being even tempered in the worst of situations, Fiona had surprised me with her passionate hatred for Ben. And Ben. Well, that ladies' man was clearly off his game because Fiona was the one woman in all of North Carolina who did not fall under his spell.

"How are things with your dad?" Max asked, wanting to switch the subject before Ben said anything truly horrible about Fiona that would draw us into their petty argument.

Ben clenched his jaw and the speedometer inched higher. "He officially fired me. Can you believe that? My own father fired me."

How to put this delicately? "Well, you were spending your entire day on the tiny houses. Can't expect him to pay you when you weren't showing up for work."

Ben grunted and I figured that was as far as the conversation would go. We all stayed blessedly quiet until Ben pulled into my lot and stopped.

"What is this?"

People milled about my property, drinks in hand, and bright streamers strung from one tree branch to another. Ben put the truck in park and waved his hand toward my building.

"This, my cousin, is your wedding reception."

I gaped out the windshield. "You did this?"

Ben shook his head on a laugh. "Oh hell no. This was all your neighbor's doing."

I thought of Angus and Edith. Fear dashed my appreciation. "Oh no."

"Oh yes." Ben threw open his door and hollered to the crowd. "They're here!"

The group all converged on the truck, every citizen I'd met since moving here, along with many others I didn't know. I helped Max out of the truck and she immediately was swept up into a round of hugs. I got a few too, with lots of pats on the back. It wasn't Mardelvia with their spiced rum and fancy confectionaries, but it was community. They'd accepted me as one of their own, not because of my name or title but because of what I'd brought to the town. The kind of community I'd been looking for all along.

Someone pressed a drink in my hand. Edith and Angus broke through the crowd–mostly because Edith was whacking people with her cane–drinks lifted high in a toast.

"To Maxine and Cavanaugh!"

We toasted to that, our arms around each other, all our neighbors around us. Someone started the music again and everyone began to break off into groups, talking and laughing and sampling the food everyone had brought for the occasion.

"Is that...cat confetti?" I squatted down and picked up a piece of shiny pink confetti in the shape of a cat. It was littered everywhere. It would be an absolute bitch to get every piece out of the dirt and weeds.

Edith used the end of her cane to tap Angus in the middle of his chest. "This dummy got the wrong confetti."

"I googled pussy confetti just like you told me to!" he groused.

Max snorted and slapped a hand to her mouth. I shook my head, biting back a grin. These two were ridiculous. And amazing.

"Thank you for the wedding reception," I said quietly, looking both of them in the eye in turn. Edith shot me a quiet smile while Angus mumbled something about charging me for resodding his grass. The two moved off and Max leaned into my side.

"Neighbors are probably a little different here in Sailfish Banks."

"You can say that again. But it's nice to be welcomed, you know? Even with pussy confetti."

Max howled with laughter and I pulled her further into the group, following her everywhere that evening. She showed off her ring and gushed about the palace. When most everyone had gone home, I loaded her up in my truck and hightailed it to her house. Bo had already told me he was staying the night at Colby's house. Which meant we had the place to ourselves.

And I'd promised my wife a baby.